advance praise for talking derby

"I'd recommend *Talking Derby* to any skater, friend or fan of roller derby. If you don't know anything about the sport, this is a great way to learn. If you're a skater, the storytelling is so good here that it jogs up all those pivotal moments that are just…everything…Great book, first of its kind, this one goes to 11."

— Bonnie D. Stroir, Assistant Coach Team U.S.A. Roller Derby, founder of San Diego Derby Dolls and LiveLoveDerby

"I loved this book! Pain Eyre beautifully captures the sights, sounds and smells of this often-misunderstood sport. From jamming through shopping malls to saying goodbye to old knee pads, the derby everyday is portrayed with humour, wit and a genuine love of the game. If you are already a roller derby junkie, or you want to learn more about this unique community, read this book!"

— Luludemon, Team Canada Roller Derby, Terminal City Rollergirl & founder of Pivotstar Apparel

"Pain Eyre nails the lingo…from snot rags to the stink of our gear. She allows a peek into the wacky world of roller derby. A refreshingly fun way of capturing the spirit of roller derby!"

— Georgia W. Tush, Team Canada Roller Derby, founder of Montreal Roller Derby & owner of Neon Skates

"*Talking Derby* is onomatopoeia heaven! Pain Eyre does a fantastic job of capturing the sights, sounds, smells, tastes, textures, and the sensuous cacophony that is roller derby. This is no leisure lifetime activity! Time warps, it's fervid and you feel alive, and there's only one way to experience it: in the here and NOW! *Talking Derby* really nails that essence, and I. Am. In. To. It."

— Scald Eagle, Rose City Rollers, Wheels of Justice & DNN Rookie of the Year 2011

"*Talking Derby* is a love letter to the toughest, coolest sport on eight wheels. From fresh meat to fresh bruises, you'll feel like you've found a derby skater's super secret diary."

— Pamela Ribon, author of *Going in Circles*, L.A. Derby Doll May Q. Holla

"*Talking Derby* is pure roiling energy. Exquisitely-written, it propels active verbs across the page like tumbling bodies and stirs the reader's yearning to be 'last one standing. Queen of the rink.'"

— Rosemary Nixon, author of *The Cock's Egg* and *Kalila*

talking derby

talking derby

talking derby

stories from a life on eight wheels

~~kate~~ "pain eyre" ~~hargreaves~~

Black Moss Press 2013

Copyright © 2013 Kate Hargreaves

Library and Archives Canada Cataloguing in Publication

Hargreaves, Kate
    Talking derby : stories from a life on eight wheels / written by Kate Hargreaves.

Short stories.
ISBN 978-0-88753-517-8

    I. Title.

PS8615.A727T36 2013   C813'.6   C2013-901171-4

Cover image by Jason Rankin & Miriah Grondin
Editing: Jineen Abuzaid, Aanand Arya, Haley Dagley, Ashly Flannery, Luke Frenette, Miriah Grondin, Lyna Hijazi, Danielle Latendresse, Shelby Maia, Sarah Passingham, Jason Rankin, Lauren Sharpe, Lauren Soul, Nicole Turner & Karly Van Puymbroeck
Design & layout: Miriah Grondin, Shelby Maia, Jason Rankin & Nicole Turner
Author photo by Brendan Adam Zwelling (bazphotography.com)
Glossary graphic by Shelby Maia
Wheel photo and derby infographic by Stephen Hargreaves

Published by Black Moss Press at 2450 Byng Road, Windsor, Ontario, N8W 3E8. Canada. Black Moss books are distributed in Canada and the U.S. by LitDistCo. All orders should be directed to LitDistCo.

Black Moss would like to acknowledge the generous financial support from both the Canada Council of the Arts and the Ontario Arts Council.

contents

five seconds	9	42	post-practice thunder
what's in a name?	11	43	achilles' heel
snot rag	13	46	greta grip
player profile	15	47	bout day
stormy	17	49	derby deeds
haunt	19	50	northern line
a vow	20	52	no sorry in derby
she's electric	21	54	ode to old knee pads
faq	22	57	playing chicken
but...there's a contest	24	58	shiner
sign scrimmage	27	60	go ahead and jump!
crack that whip	28	62	jam stopper
slideshow	29	63	day off
border crossing	30	65	dance off
gear bath	32	67	spartans
ice time	33	68	bearing bath
give blood, play derby	34	70	price on my head
velcro kiss	36	72	take a knee
office crossovers	37	74	snapshot
what's your number?	38	77	appendix: roller derby 101
dress code	39	81	glossary
you want me to eat what?	41	86	acknowledgements

to my derby widow

five seconds

Stale air weighs down the warehouse. 50 feet above our heads, the grid of fans struggles to manufacture a breeze. A zebra skates over to the door, grabs the iron handle and lurches backward to roll it open along metal tracks. The sun stretches his shadow across the dusty concrete, toe stoppers to helmet, as he stands between warehouse and daylight.

A whistle blasts and 20 women slide into centre-track on their knee pads. "Take off your helmets, cool down, get some water!" Coach Ryan Ginger, shirt sweat-dark, stuck to his back, snatches the jammer and pivot panties from the floor and tosses them to skaters who throw back quick sips of water, re-clip helmets under their chins. I stretch the black jammer star over my helmet.

Black shirts versus White line up on the track. Mary Kate Smashley grabs a white shirt from the equipment room pinny bag and throws it over her head, XL on her XS frame. *Plumbing Experts. Call Us.* In the pack, Lily Bad wears a ripped white tee over her own black shirt, tied in the front.

Sweat crawls down my neck into my black tank top. *Five seconds!* I step up on my toe stoppers, ready to start running. Someone's chatting on the other side of the warehouse: four or five figures in the doorway, pointing over at our track. *Screee!* The whistle releases me and Smashley into the pack. *Umph*—I take a hit from the white team pivot, trip and spin out on my knee pads. Smashley grabs a whip off her blocker and makes it out of the pack, zebra pointing her out as lead while she sprints back around the track. I scramble up and dodge white-shirt blockers, grab at my teammates' hips. See a hole and take three quick strides. I'm out, but Smashley's almost ready to start scoring. *Team Black to the front!* I'm slipping out on the corners of the track, crossing over in quick strides to catch her. She hits the pack, picks up two points on a couple of black-shirt blockers lingering at the back and taps her hips with both hands. Four whistles. Two points for Team White.

Jammers and pivots tug panties off helmets, toss them at Ryan, and roll over to the "bench" to grab some water. Wipe sweat from faces and necks with shirt-bottoms. There's no bench, just a line of water bottles and sports drinks against a wall. Team White on one side of the leaky water fountain, Team Black on the other.

"Take a break. Let's talk about what happened there. What went wrong, what—"

Roller...no, not blades...What are they...

"What? Talk louder!"

Thought this...empty...skating

"I SAID. WHAT WENT WRONG? WHAT WENT—"

More evening strollers lean in the doorway, chatter over Ryan's speech. A man pulls a camera out. Flash. I duck out of the talk on why Team Black's wall fell apart and why White should have slowed the pack down.

"Hi folks. Can I help you?"

The man with the camera lets it hang down on the strap around his neck. "Sorry, but, what *is* this?"

I pull my mouthguard out, slurping off spit, and tuck it into the top of my tights. A slow breath readies the spiel I recite to every person who asks why my knees are purple, why I can't make it to their party Saturday night, or why my phone's ringing with a call from "Smash" or "Crabby." Behind me, a zebra calls *five seconds* and the whistle blows for the next jam. "This...this is roller derby. Here's how it works..."

what's in a name?

What about Helen Killer?

Taken.

Penelope Bruise?

Gone.

Margaret Scratcher?

That one's free. No surprise there.

Why? I bet she'd have been great at roller derby. Politics is a contact sport.

Kim Slam-bell?

That's awful. What about something book-ish? Who do you read?

Sylvia Plath? Sylvia Wrath? Wait, that's taken too.

Killvia Plath?

Claimed. Maybe go a bit more historic. Emily Break-inson?

That's a stretch. Dorian Slay?

Yes! Wait, she plays in Missouri.

Malice in Wonderland?

Definitely taken.

Hermione Danger? Lady Slaughter-ly? Elizadeath Bennett?

I like that last one. How about Pain Austen?

Perfect.

Damn, she plays for Burning River.

I've got it. Pain Eyre.

I bet it's taken.

It's punny.

And short. But what if the announcer didn't pay attention in English lit? Here's Pain I-rie on the jammer line. Pain Ire. Pain Airy. Pain Ear.

Pain Eyre. Claim it. Own it. Now all you need is a number.

A number, sure. And a pair of skates.

snot rag

I arrived at practice with:
    a fever (100.2 degrees)
    a leaky nose
    my snot rag.

I've tried toilet paper, which is always a disaster: skating laps with a disintegrating wad of half-ply in one fist, dropping shreds all over the track. Sick of the TP mess, I grabbed the bandana from my skate bag and blew. Introducing: the snot rag. When I skated in denim shorts, I tucked the hanky in my back pocket like a mechanic. Pocketless, I shove it in my waistband, green cotton flapping like I'm playing capture the flag. Except everyone knows to NEVER touch the green bandana if it falls. It practically flashes *BIOHAZARD*.

          *   *   *

Pace line: we skate two arm lengths apart, but the skaters beside me estimate longer limbs and leave me plenty of space to sneeze and blow. After 50 laps and water, we move on to sideways skating. *Point your toes out. Straighter than that. Lean on the wall if you have to.*

My knees knock when I jog. I crumple shoes, wearing down only the insides. No dancer's turnout here, in toe-shoes, sneakers or skates. I tried practicing at the bus stop or while washing dishes, inch-by-inching feet outwards waiting in line for the ladies room, frying eggs at the stove, blow-drying my hair. Tonight, my pigeon-toes must turn out and skate at the same time.

I try gliding on one foot and dropping the other skate down. A perfect smooth t-stop. Both feet on the floor, push out and I turn in a little circle. Crabby Apple rolls past in perfect straight sideways strides.

Is there a clock in this warehouse? What time is it and can we do something, anything else? We can play endless jammer and I'll jam the entire time. The whole league can do a hitting drill on me and me alone. We could do thirty sets of burpees and push-ups. Forty. Plank for an hour. Anything. *Anything* but sideways skating. Greta Grip glides around the apex, heel-to-heel. I catapult my water bottle against the bricks and call it a practice. No, no I don't, but I'm back to my first month of skating outside in the square, ass kissing concrete every four steps, skates and legs un-belonging to the rest of me. I sniffle and rag my nose, damp and peeling. Honk, snort and glide on one foot. Step step drip skid.

Four whistles mean stop: scrimmage time. Use what you've learned in a jam: nasal evacuation and one foot glides. It's my power jam but my stomach is sloshing. My eyelids sweat and my nose trickles as I round the track to get back into the pack. I whip out my snot rag on the straightaway and blow.

"Nice one!" Greta laughs from the White Team bench. Am I the first jammer to blow my nose on a power jam? I pick up a couple points before a hit from the inside jolts my head back and an arc of mucus escapes my nostrils, scrimmage shirt bound. Knee pads and nylon on concrete, hanky in hand, I slam my hands to hips to call the jam off from my knees. I'm ready to lie down and close my eyes, cheek pressed against concrete, but I drag myself back to the bench, gulp down some water, grab my snot rag. Blow.

player profile

*fill in all sections and return by Tuesday

Name: Pain Eyre, my team calls me Pain

Number: 1847

Primary Position: aspiring triple-threat (jammer/blocker/sometimes pivot)

Derby-versary: August 2010

Age: 20-something

I fell for derby because: Um…

Loves: Mr. Rochester, dark and stormy nights, endurance drills

Hates: Sideways skating, passive offense, loose stoppers

I fell for derby because: ~~I needed to exercise and hated the gym~~

Off-skates alter ego: paper, ink and spines: designing, shelving, promoting, editing, writing.

Derby secret weapon: hits harder than a three-volume novel

Frequently in the Sin Bin for: accidentally egregious apex jumps, cougaring

Usually screaming: at everyone. *Inside! Outside! Slow down! Get a goat! To the front! Bridge me! Bridge her! Faster! Slow down!*

I fell for derby because: ~~I saw a wheat pasted poster and thought~~ maybe I could do ~~that~~

Favourite piece of gear: soccer shin guards from eighth grade

Crap in your gear bag: tensor bandages, duct tape, medical tape, sports tape, three pairs of socks, two extra mouthguards, four old bout programs, half a melted protein bar

The *real* reason you fell for derby: ~~On TV, derby was roller skates, fishnet tights,~~

~~and tattoos. As thrilling as that sounded, I possessed none of the above and my hometown was derby-free. Then I saw a flyer—~~

Injuries: minor damage to: knees, elbows, nose, ear, friendships, cheek, ass, ankles, wallet, neck, shoulder, ego, hip, groin, calf, fingers, toes

Try again: ~~I showed up at the first practice and sat on a rock ledge. Watched fifteen girls wobble around the square. Pitch forward onto kneepads. Tapped my feet on the cement and itched for a pair of skates~~

Look for me on the track: a foot above the other skaters

Biggest derby myth: That we're just girls going in circles looking cute. Strap on some gear and skate a three-hour practice. Then we'll see who looks "cute"

So about that time you fell for derby: Laced into my first pair of skates. Stumbled onto the chalk "track," lock-knees and tippy-bird stance. Sat suicide for my first bout a week later. A bench-mark. A challenge. A refusal to be terrible forever—

Anything else? I wobbled beside fifteen other skaters. Skaters who snagged skills faster. Tomahawked, t-stopped, transitioned. Who cheered at bouts beside me. Baked cupcakes and sold raffle tickets to pay our rink rent. Pulled me up off the cement. Taught and re-taught me footwork. I fell for derby. For skates. For crossovers and jumps. For zebras, officials and trainers. For my derby family. For bouts and scrimmages. For push-ups and cardio. For sweat and compression pants. For toe stoppers, jammer starts and hip checks—

Your theme song: "Heads Will Roll"

stormy

Hoodie, jacket, gloves, toque. I sling my gear bag over my shoulder, toe the kickstand on my bike and wheel it toward the apartment door. Ivy bangs the windows, cold air rushing through the cracks around the air conditioner and the sky is one of those shades of green I'd paint chip pick for a nice accent wall.

I usually roll up at the warehouse in all weather, wind, rain and a couple feet of snow melting through sneakers at red lights. The thick beach cruiser tires have enough grip to keep me on the road and pedaling a heavy bike hard against the wind means my legs warm up before I even lace my skates.

Tonight, standing on the porch clutching the handlebars, I call it 1 for the weather, 0 for Pain Eyre. A recycling bin hurtles down the road and the wind tugs at my toque. I un-pocket my phone and text Becky Check, see if she's up for rescuing a derby damsel in distress. When she pulls up outside I make a quick dash to the kitchen, grab a Tupperware of lentil curry and run out into the wind. Roller derby ride-share, swapping snacks for storm shelter.

*   *   *

Eight wheels squeal as I hockey stop at the edge of the track for some water. I pull out my snot rag, honk my nose, tuck the damp bandana into my tights and skate to the back of the warehouse where we're lining up for a blocking drill. I catch Becky's glance, pause, tap the side of my helmet and point to a line of jammers, motion a block with my hips and point to the other line: blockers. I make the signs for skate, fast, and jammer. Becky nods.

It's an understatement to say my ASL needs work. I mix up P and Q when I fingerspell and my most-used signs are "slower" and "repeat, sorry." I can remember useless phrases I learned online but grandmothers, church, and cats don't tend to come up often in derby.

"After this we'll do 20 in 5 as a pack," Ryan Ginger yells from centre-track. I make the referee signal for pack and draw a circle in the air. Pack, laps, 5 minutes—what's 20? I sign 2, then a 0. Or is that a C?

Becky raises an eyebrow and points to Ryan. "He's crazy, 200 laps in five minutes!" She laughs and signs 20. "You're learning, it's okay!" and throws a friendly hip check on her way by me to grab her water. Add to my practice list: footwork, Ps and Qs, hip checks, numbers.

haunt

1, 2, 3 TURN AROUND. Red hand prints. Is that blood on the wall? HELP ME! smeared across the inside of the door. Then: Ex-haunted house. Ex-armouries. Now: our skate warehouse. Iva Sling pulls her phone from her waistband and flashlights as we inch through the horror-movie dark. A pile of artificial spiderwebs in the corner. Dried cans of red paint. Blood splatter spoiled.

Red light leaks under the door: end of the hall. Iva's wrist-guard Velcro catches mine. *Holding hands for more than three seconds makes a multiplayer block.* Hinges creak cliché as we toe-stopper tip-toe into the glow of fast food neon casting red across the floor.

Iva rolls to the window. Pedestrians sludge past below in hoods and hats, heads down, shielding faces from the wind. If they looked up and saw a pale face peering from an empty warehouse—There's a double-take but she rolls away before they look back. A ghost vanishing into a haunted house.

Ghosts don't like roller derby. The living are too noisy to spook with creaking doors and sudden bangs. They stay hidden until the women with their *inside! outside! plow!* yells and whistles slam the door for the night. Borrow a pair of rental skates from the equipment room and glide around the track.

First lesson for the jammers: slipping through walls.

a vow

Dear Iva,

We've been skating together over seven months now. Seven beautiful months of endurance drills, after-party pizza, and bruise comparisons. We have sweated alongside one another, locked wheels and fallen together. Your skate left a heart-shaped bruise on my bum like the wheel-mark you've left on my heart. Our toenails have fallen off together, we've wrapped our feet in sports tape together. We've pushed each other to skate faster, harder, to try that jump or that hit or that footwork one more time. You smell like vinegar and I reek of eggs. You're always willing to share a protein bar or a banana at half-time. To share frustrations at skaters dropping out of drills. Not showing up for practice. Packages of make-up wipes before the after-party. We've shared a couple wins and many, many, losses. Four trips to the emergency room. To the fracture clinic. To the drugstore to buy band-aids and arnica bruise cream. We've shared our derby lives, on the bench and the track, in the sin bin and the bar, in limping and in health. I've thought bout long and hip check hard. I'd like to share my derby life with you. I promise to lend a skate tool and an ear. To shake each others' shoulders and yell "head in the game!" and cheer the loudest during bout-day intros. I promise to never leave you without a partner in a pace line, never to leave you without a ride to the bout. As your derby wife I promise to be the one who rides in the ambulance beside you and backs you up when you appeal a call (even if you *did* cut the track). With this skate tool, be my partner in grime. With these bearings, I thee wed.

she's electric

Buzz. Buzz. Buzz. Buzz. Fresh meat practice. My mission: to instruct new skaters on the art of booty blocking. The result: limping couch to bathroom three hours later to wipe the dry blood crusting under my nose and a TENS machine cranked to 7.5.

At free skate last week I clipped my own wheel and torqued a leg out. I pushed off the floor to stand and—*auuuuuugh*. Something popped. Gotta stretch: gripping a window ledge and swinging my leg straight out and up, and out and up. Down onto the concrete, butterfly stretch. Stripper stretch. Skeleton key. Hurdler stretch. Repeat.

Buzz. Buzz. Electro pulses jolt my muscles and thigh skin tremors, twitches under the pulse-pads and goes still. Twitch. Twitch. Buzz. Buzz. I turn the knob up to 9 and *ow shit!* snatch it back down again.

One chiropractic adjustment, four sets of stretches a day, heat packs, cold packs, ibuprofin and five days of flinching putting on socks. I thought I'd be loose and limber to skate tonight. I even hiked over to Sobey's limp-free. The chiro calls it a nasty muscle pull and recites a prescription to stay off skates and rest a while. Define "a while."

Time to lace up. Hop, skip and *augggh*. Tonight's remedy was taking it easy. Define "taking it easy." Every time the coach yelled sprint, I sprinted. When he yelled plow, I plowed wide and low. And when it was time to do crossovers clockwise, left leg over right, I crossed over, every step grinding teeth to mouthguard. Buzz. Buzz. I'd jump around a bit, chase the jammer, step out to hit her, then *ooooh god*.

Taking it easy. A fresh meat lesson in booty blocking later, my hip's in knots and my nose is bleeding. Positional blocking 101: a freshie stood up straight, me skating low right behind her, and *wham!* Shoulder, meet nose. Tonight I glimpse my first blood. Buzz. Buzz. Electro-pulses up to 8, sniffling through a bruised septum.

faq

So you play roller derby?
Do you punch each other in the face?
or wrestle?
on the track?
in the mud?
in jello?
I hear you don't wear pants
just cute little uniforms
like lingerie football
is that true?
So are you single?
or into girls?
This isn't just a lesbian thing, is it?
Can I watch you practice?
I need to meet some women.
I could ref; it's just like hockey, right?
So you think you're tough now?
some sort of badass?
throw elbows?
ever got a black eye?
fishnet burns?
like that girl from *Juno*?

on those old-fashioned skates?
like in the '70s?
I used to watch it back then;
those ladies were rough.
Do you stage who wins?
throw tables on the track?
pull hair?
rip clothes?
Do you wear helmets?
have a pin-up calendar?
a trading card?
a phone number?
How much money do you make?
That still exists? Roller derby?
Where's the ball?

but...there's a contest

Ibuprofin. Gulp. I toss my water bottle into my gear bag's side pocket, zip it up and throw the strap over one shoulder. I slam the front door and sidestep down three porch steps. Right leg limp. My skates have been stinking up the closet for over a week and it's been two since the initial pull. I cross fingers and toes that my hip flexor flexes tonight. What better way to find out than three hours of travel tryouts?

But, I'm going to take it easy. Crabby rolls her eyes from the driver's seat.

"Sure you are."

"Seriously, I'm going to take it easy."

"But…" Crabby raises one eyebrow. "But…there's a contest: first skater to 32 laps in 5 minutes. Winner gets a free Team Canada derby tee."

"I'm going to take it easy."

I know I won't be able to skate my 25 laps and coast. 25 in 5, the much-groaned-about roller derby staple: 25 standard track laps in five minutes or less. My last attempt maxed out at 31, and with a free shirt on the finish line, why not try? Crabby reminds me that there are several reasons why not, including a recovering muscle pull, an impending holiday scrimmage, and the risk of limping my way through the Christmas break. A challenge is a challenge is a challenge.

Crabby presses the buzzer and the thick wood door swings open. Mary Kate Smashley steps out from behind, sporting a paper number eight taped to the front and back of her helmet. I grab number 16, dump my bag by the wall and drop down to the floor for a good hip stretch. Tight, but no knots. No limp, a slight tug. 32 laps? Maybe.

We hockey stop. We pack skate. We plow. We jump. We block. We recycle. And then, the last water break before 25 in 5. *Five skaters at a time, spread out!* I'm assigned the second shift so I grab my water and try to guzzle before my five minute sprint-a-thon.

"Pain, can you count for Iva?"

I sit down and hurdler stretch on the inside of the track facing out towards the wife. In between sips of water as she passes: "five laps, awesome! Great pace! Keep it up!" and "Push it, push it! Only a minute left! Finish strong!" As the thirty seconds-to-go mark breezes by, I stand and start to shake out my legs. "Go go go! One more lap, you can do it!" The five-minute whistle blows; some slide to the ground as the coach yells "skate it off slowly, don't let your muscles seize up! Next five on the track!"

Damn! I coast over to Ryan "I'msorryIgottapeedoIhavetimeI'llberightback!" I clatter into the bathroom, pulling off my wrist guards, and toss them outside the door as I roll onto the damp tile. Washing my hands, my name bounces around the warehouse, *PAIN! PAIN!* I stumble down the bathroom step. Ears burning, I strap on my wrist guards, sprint to the track—the whistle goes and I'm off running on my toe stops.

At the minute-mark, I've only hit six and a half laps and I'm slowing. My quads are already howling and side-stepping *inside!* to pass a slower skater tugs at my hip. Coach Ryan is counting laps in a low voice, but as I hit 10 and then 15 well before three minutes—*Go, go, hit 32!* I pass the 25 mark, thighs screaming, chest pumping. Gulping air, I eek out *inside!* and screech up behind other skaters. Choppy stride crossovers, I'm bent too far at the waist. 30 seconds to go, I'm at 29 laps, desperate to cross out a few more. Thighs, calves quaking, *ten* and I finish lap 31, *six*, heading toward Ryan Ginger, *two* my marker for 32. He blows the whistle. 31 and three quarters, goddammit! Two seconds away. Two. damn. seconds.

Hands on knees I coast centre-track, spin the cap off my water. The last drips slide off the plastic. Shit. *Screeeee!* A whistle catches me on my refill as Ryan waves me over to the jammer line for an impromptu race. Win: get the shirt. Three minutes recovery and a two-lap sprint. Against him. Can't I just admit defeat by quads and concrete floor? No shirt, no race? Cut off one sleeve for the missing quarter lap? Toe-stopper standing, a blister sizzles along the edge of my big toe. A zebra blows a quick whistle blast but Ryan jumps off the line early, false starts and yields me advantage. I swing past onto the inside line, hug the apex, boots leaning hard on loose trucks. Blister digging against damp leather, I stagger down the straightaway and cross the line with Ryan steps behind. A free shirt on the back of a false start, I grab for my empty bottle and drift toward the fountain for some water. *Screeeee!* Another whistle. *Scrimmage time!* Someone tosses me the jammer panty. I bend my knee and pull my leg up to my chest. Hip twinges. Toe burns. Water sloshes in my belly. *Five seconds!* Tryouts aren't over yet.

sign scrimmage

"Vampire Arms! 'Relax' looks like vampire arms!"

Pens scritchscratch workbook paper. Vampire arms, move down. Next word: "water." I know this one. "W tap chin". We're speeding through the signs and my handwriting slopes down the page. "Hop?" Is that what I wrote? Is "hop" the same sign as "jump?" Two fingers springing from a flat palm. But this says— "Help." Right. But what did I write for "hit?" "Index and middle finger claws. Tap together." And "fast?" Becky Check raises the flash card and the room gestures wildly. "Fast" is—I know to draw my hand up my other wrist for "slow," but what the hell is "fast"? Becky points to the bristol board at the front of the room. In photos, Crabby Apple and Lily Bad act out each sign, duct tape across their mouths. FAST: Lily points both index fingers out in the photo, bends them toward her in the next shot. Fast. That's it. But I've got to sign it fast too!

"What's the sign for 'hot?'" Iva fans herself with her workbook. Twenty sweaty skaters cramming a tiny community centre. Black and white scrimmage shirts, room divided down the middle, Team Black huddles before giving each answer. We're off-skates, but there's still a bout to win. We picked teams and stretched our arms and hands before we began. Deaf culture quiz, question 1: no, Deaf people do not get special parking spots. 2: Deaf people are usually born to hearing parents. 3: Facial expressions are a major part of ASL.

"Scrimmage!" Becky pulls the flash card for "jammer" and every person in the room rushes to tap the side of her head. "Skate." Forty hands glide back and forth with the sign for roller skating. "Game." Thumbs up, tap knuckles together. "Team." A letter "T" with both hands. A complete circle. Becky points both index fingers and taps her fists one on top of the other. Correct. Applause. Forty hands wave the air.

crack that whip

Beeeeeeeeep. I snatch the beanbag out of the microwave and try to rest it on my shoulder. Wrong spot. A little further forward. Heat soaks into my neck muscles for a moment then—*Thwack.* The bag hits the floor. I bend and oh god my back. Legs. Quads. Calves. I pull myself up like someone four times my age, 80 plus years grinding my bones and tuck the hot bag under my chin telephone-style. Perfect. This morning, I rolled in bed and—neck. Stuck. Crunch. It twisted and nodded and turned last night but at 9AM a jolt shuddered through my shoulders. Stretching my calves and quads slowly, I perched on the edge of my mattress and pulled jeans over my ankles, knees, hips and, *ow*. I forgot my hipbone, accessorized with a blood-stain band-aid couched by a growing green splotch. I gingerly wiggled hips into jeans, zip and popped an antibiotic for this sludgy sinus cold. *Aaaaachooo!* A sneeze snaps my head forward. Yesterday's tournament replays on my body with every twitch.

*   *   *

"I totally thought you weren't getting up." Iva taps my shoulder from behind our bench. She watched me jam the first jam of our first game in our first tournament of our first real season through parted fingers. Two grand slams behind me, the purple jammer lined me up, got a shoulder on my chest, and can openered me like baked beans over a fire pit. As my legs flew forward and tailbone cracked the floor, I felt my head racing toward tile. *Fwack!* Gotta keep jamming! I sprang up on toe stoppers, caught the pack and panted through a couple more laps while my blockers walled the purple jammer out of the way.

On the bench Lily suggests neck stretches and ice. "If you don't feel it now, you'll feel it tomorrow." Two more bouts and the only pain I'm feeling is a thundering stomach and hipbone tile burn. My skin records a superman fall onto interlocking tile, protruding joints and hinges. I paid with a chunk of flesh. Yesterday's band-aid under shorts is today's green bloom. *If you don't feel it now, you'll feel it tomorrow.* Hot bag hits the floor. I bend at the back, the knees, neck stiff. My first game, first jam, first grand slam, first whiplash of the season.

slideshow

Cheeks flush. Forehead lined with effort. Mascara smear. Eyes squinting straight ahead. God, my jammer face is not pretty. Click. Next. Click. Next: a slideshow of photos from our most recent bout: Click. Next. Click: nose-wrinkle and gritted teeth.

We knew they'd be a tough team: a week before the bout I met our opponents via online slideshow. Black and white headshots of sturdy women staring down the camera. A black eye. Fake? My own league photo caught me mid-laugh, lunging forward, mouth agape and eyes closed. I guess I could be screaming. Click. Next. Click. Next. Mouthguard digging bottom lip. Cheekbones pressing up under eyes. Click. Next. Click. Click. Hair jutting lank and sweaty from the front of my helmet, mouth open and panting, cheeks blotchy. Click. Pulped between two Purple Team players, both sets of hips swinging toward my gangly frame. Face flush, one foot off the ground gnashing mouthguard to teeth. Just two. More. Steps. Gotta push past the hit. Not on film: turn three of the track where a hip check takes me up and off my feet, a backwards somersault into the suicide seating and earns me a wheel-shaped welt from kicking myself in the ass. Not on film: sliding on one knee into our bench after two jams in a row, grasping for a full water bottle. Floored and floored again by blockers twice my size.

Click. Next. Slideshow: Derby World Cup. Smack Daddy jammed against Team Sweden and gave the announcers chills: *she looks like she's going to eat everybody! I think she just swallowed her mouthguard.* Click. I only notice the faces in the photo recap. I watched from the stands with thousands of fans, zoomed in on feet, hips, and shoulders. Juke, jam and block. Click. Skaters glaring down the track off the line, gritting teeth against mouthguard plastic, dragging lead legs to standing. Click. Creasing brows to push through. One. Last. Lap. Click. Bout paint cheek smudge. Click. Girls skating in circles. Click. Roller derby is not pretty.

border crossing

"Where are you going?"

"Speed class."

"What?"

Acid sweat-stink wafts from the back of the SUV.

"Roller skating. Derby. We're going to a speed class."

"Pop the trunk."

The guard strolls around the back of the truck and opens the hatch. Sweat, diesel and idle fumes.

"*Worship Skatin'?*"

My helmet. The guard lifts it by the greying used-to-be-yellow straps and thumbs the peeling stickers that cover its scuffs.

"*Talk derby to me. Keep calm and hit your friends. Blood is the new black.*"

She snorts, tosses the helmet back into the hatch. Thud. Wobble.

Iva leans toward the back seat. "At least she didn't mention the bumper sticker."

The guard tugs the straps on one of the other bags. *Zzzzzzip.*

"Oh god, Crabby is that yours?"

Rotting Big Macs. Wet sneakers. Sweaty boxers. "What the hell did you pack?"

The guard tugs the bag open, coughs. Tight-lipped, she straightens her gloves and hovers a hand. Damp knee pads snag wrist guard velcro. A stray skate tool clinks out onto the trunk lining. *Zzzziiippp*. Cough. She slams the hatch. Litter box. Vinegar. Stale fritos. Gasoline.

Back in her booth, she thumbs the passports.

"Can't you skate at home?"

"Hockey season. No rinks." Lily Bad takes the Q and A from the wheel. "It's ice in August and no looking back for eight months."

Iva drums the dash. Cups a hand over nose and mouth. Curry and beer store empties.

"Sunglasses off. Which one of you is Jill?"

Jill? I don't even know any Jill. Then again, no one's legal name is Iva Sling.

Iva hits the power window button and waves, sunglasses on her head.

"Catherine?"

Crabby?

The guard thumbs the passports, hands them off to Lily.

"Have a nice skate ladies. Be sure to stay low and watch out for that slick third turn. And say hi to Jackie Fight for me."

Lily pulls the truck into gear and rolls out onto the highway.

The aroma of wrist guards and feet starts to build again in the heat. A loose skate tool clanks in the trunk.

gear bath

Crabby Apple calls to check, "is your bathtub free? I've got a fresh box of Borax." She turns up with a plaid backpack, Velcro gear straps sticking through the zippers. They catch on my corduroy couch. *frrrrriiiiiiip*. Tap runs warm water. No bubble bath, candles or incense here, just soap scum stains. Crabby dumps half a box of Borax and white powder clumps at the bottom of the tub. She rolls one sleeve up, hand in the water *splash* to break the powder up. I drag my duffle bag in from the hall, unzip, and un-Velcro knee pad, knee pad, two gaskets, wrist guard, helmet padding, elbow pad, wrist guard, elbow pad, and ankle brace. The tap runs, more Borax white powder on black pads while I dunk the straps and plastic caps. Crabby turns her bag on end, dumps. Pads clatter. Sweat, hot water, Borax, steam. More powder for good measure (except we never measure, just dump). Slosh the gear under, clunk the tap off and *oh god, the water's going green.* Gear bath swamp steams.

Forty-five minutes (coffee, half an episode of *Buffy,* kitchen sweep).

Elbow pad grabs a gasket, knee pad hooks onto another and the water: brown. Mouse fur brown like my roots and the ring around the edge of the tub as the grimy water flows down. Crabby refills her bag, drip dripping through the lining to hang pads on her clothesline. Green/yellow sponge coarse side down, I scrub with bleach and Vim to fade the tub rings, but gear gunk lingers. My pads dry on the window radiator, spread out and dripping off strap ends onto couch corduroy. Kitchen coffee and toast cut into stale sweat. Grime sticks to the tub. Stench sleeps in the seams.

ice time

The great Canadian Tim Horton's commercial—backyard ice rink snow suit kid pushing around a plastic chair on a wobbly pair of hockey skates—never happened for me. I never shoveled goalie creases. There was no concession stand hot chocolate and figure eights. On grade school skate day, I had to find a matching pair of donated rentals in the kindergarten closet the morning of, board-clutching while the hockey kids snowed my tilting ankles. Mum and Dad didn't skate. *No one ice skates in England.* I nodded along to tips from figure skating moms and hockey dads who skate-laced drippy-nose eight-year-olds at the town rink. *Bend your knees, kid!*

Tonight's practice may as well be at the arena. My wheels have zero traction. When Ryan yells sprint, I try to dig in and push out a few fast crossovers to give myself some track space. I drift through the turn, arms wide like I'm casting a spell, and almost spill onto the concrete, left leg slipping under and off the track. *Hey coach! When's the last time we Coked the floors?* Wheels squeal at both turns and *ohhhhh shit!* and *sorry! sorry!* as skaters slide sideways into one another.

We'll sugar it after the holidays. Coke's too pricey. SPRINT! I clip my crossovers short, half-running down the track and hit the corner hard. My wheels *screeeeeeeeee* around the turn. Should have swapped out to a softer wheel. Or had my ice skates sharpened.

give blood, play derby

"What's my time?" I have to win. 32 in 5. Pushing out faster harder crossovers every practice. "So far? About seven minutes." Damn. I must have blood like ketchup. Greta finished in under four and a half and I'm barely flowing at seven. Crabby's in the chair next to me ready to be needled. Give blood, play derby takes on a whole new meaning when a nurse—needle, blood bags and tubes in hand—starts disinfecting your arm. I wiggle my fingers. Come on! Let's go!

*   *   *

"Roll up your sleeves. And the other side?" Interview room one. Connect the purple splotches down my arms.

"The bruises…I'm with the roller derby team." Wrong kind of track marks. Right kind of track marks. Last night's scrimmage smudges my skin. The nurse nods me to roll down my sleeves and escort my pile of tubes and empty blood bags into the waiting area. Tap tap tap. Tap tap. My fingers drum the chair arm, stomach whirring like before a bout. Crabby walks out of the nurse's room, bags in hand, face as green as her hair.

"You step on the track against girls twice your size. A little blood? No problem." A thin needle in the arm versus a wheel to the ass. A bony hip to the thigh. A shoulder to the ribs. An elbow to the nose. A— nip to the arm and the needle slides in. The nurse hums and draws samples, barcoding tubes as my blood slips down lines into a clear plastic bag. How do I make this go faster? Squeeze fist. Open. Close. Open. Close. Wiggling fingers to the rhythm of the Phil Collins song on the radio. Against all odds? The beat of the weather man's forecast. Open. Close. *Tonight we'll see showers.* Open. *With a forty percent chance.* Close. *of thunderstorms.* Blood bag tipping back and forth and barely full, I'm wiggling and clenching my hand fast and faster, arm stiff to the shoulder. Keep it still. Open. Close. Tubing pulls against arm crook skin.

Crabby's getting the alcohol swab treatment. Then comes—

"So do you know it's going to be 92 degrees tomorrow? Rain in the afternoon too." An empty blood bag. A needle. More pressing than weather. "I once went on a date to a blood donor clinic. Made him weak in the knees." A quick draw of breath and "that wasn't too bad, right?" Now the contest is really on. Wiggle wiggle wiggle, bag still half empty. Or half full. What time is it? How much longer is this going to take? Three commercial breaks with the news ticker flashing the *TSX is up and the DOW is down. Construction slowing traffic down on the east side this afternoon.* Needle-free Crabby heads toward the cookies and juice, and I'm still trickling. A nurse passes me a stress ball to squeeze. Open. Close. Open.

"Almost there, just a bit more."

Beeeeeep. "So what was my time?" Eight minutes? Nine maybe?

"Eleven minutes forty seconds." Blood like old honey. Like Cheez Whiz. Like skating 12 in 5, never mind 25. I catch Crabby over at the cookie table. Pierce an apple juice box and survey the selection: Oreos. Sugar cookies. Ginger snaps. A contest I can win. How many cookies can one person eat in five minutes? Strawberry shortcake in each hand, it's time to find out.

velcro kiss

Lukewarm water runs over my ears. Damn this shower. Damn this apartment. "Who used all the hot water?" I tilt my head back and my cheek burns. *Ow.* Hair in knots dripping in front of the mirror, I drag my fingers across my face and trace a small red patch under my eye and a thin scratch trailing down my cheek.

Why do I always have to get hit in the face?

We were back on our sticky floor tonight, skating alongside the fresh meat, panting through a partner drill. Follow your partner through the pace line. Weave between the pairs. Stay together. Go. The freshie next to me toe-stopper trips, loses derby stance, flails her arms wide. Wristguard: 1. Pain's face: 0. Velcro cheek kisses. "Sorry!"

"Pain, did someone hit you in the face?"

"Pain, there's some red stuff on your face?"

"Hey Pain, jeeze, what happened to your cheek?"

"Did you get punched in the face again?"

Yeah, yeah. Skate on. Lily Bad lines us up for suicide drills. From your stomach, up skating, pushups, back to the line, sit ups, back to the line, plank, back to the line, next skater.

"You're next Pain. God, did you know you cut your face?"

I limped into class last September in sandals, a tensor bandage around one ankle. Wrapped my knee under floral wedding tulle. Bruises and scratches daubing strapless arms. Parents pointing out derby souvenirs.

I slap some moisturizer on my cheeks. The scratch sucks it up and bites. I root around in my makeup bag. Eyeliner. Shadow. Pencil shavings. Tweezers. *Damn.* Out of cover stick.

office crossovers

Can't they make chairs with more padding? Shift left. Shift right. Adjust jeans waistband. Office seat squeaks as I wiggle, lean back, cross and uncross my legs. Crossover. Uncrossover. One cheek twinges as I shift too far right. Bruise appraisal in the morning mirror. Nothing yet. But it's coming.

At practice: "Did you see my badge of honour?" Lily yanks down one side of her shorts and shows a purple and black welt the size of a fist. Edges fray yellow. "And it's still growing!" Shift left. Shift right. *Ow.* Two o'clock. Three more hours. Shift right.

At practice, I threw a hip check and collided with, "oh god your hips are so bony!" Crabby's counterblock, a clattering of bones. Hip-on-hip, like clacking wristguards together. Track-side we shake inside legs out. Rub the pang through compression pants. *Okay, now switch sides!* Praise Quadzilla. Tricep stretch. Shoulders. Quads. Hurdler stretch. *Ow.* Hip meets concrete. Thrums. I rock onto the other side.

Key in the front door, I dump my gear bag and drop from standing into couch cushions. *Ow.* In bed, I stretch and roll. Belly. Side. Back. Morning mirror and still no bruise. But it's there. Killing time, muscle deep, edging toward skin surface. Shift left. Shift right. Adjust chair. Lean back. Shift right. Crossover.

what's your number?

"I don't know if it's the marker or your arm." Ten minutes before the starting whistle, we scratch our upper arms with thick black permanent marker. I trace over and over Greta's number but it still disappears in the flowers climbing her bicep. I can't tell if the warm-up sweat's diluting the ink or the jungle just hides it. Either way, her number's not showing and if she skates that way, it's a pointless minute in the box. Becky Check tosses over a fatter marker and I paper-towel off Greta's arms, sweat staining dark patches on the napkin. Crumple. Toss. Try again. "Iva, can you number me?" She uncaps another marker.

"1847 right?" Scrawls a large number 1 a few inches onto my arm. Then an 8. I can feel the marker moving closer to my armpit. The 4 comes out half the size, and the 7 is tiny and tickles as she squooshes it into the last inch before it disappears under my arm.

"You need a shorter number. Or bigger arms."
I didn't factor in bicep circumference when I picked my number, the year of publication for *Jane Eyre*. Nerdy or not, our league fields two number 5s but only one 1847.

Iva pens my other arm. I could be p. 3, p. 6. Two simple characters bold on my skinny bicep. Vol. 2 is too long. Ch. 3. Ch. 8.

We push out pushups at practice. One lap. One pushup. One lap. Two pushups. Up to ten and back down again. I start on my toes and take a knee on the first set of nine. My arms wobble under my weight. A shorter number or bigger arms. Lily pumps out military-style pushups without a grimace while I start back down at nine and grunt with each push. Elbows bending further and further from the ground. Shoulder-shake. Bigger arms or a shorter number. Four. Push. Three. Push. Two. Push. p.1.

dress code

More pink than red, really. Barely even a scratch. I run my hand across the rosy warm skin of my upper arms, trace a faint 18 and part of a 7 in greying marker. In the shower I loaded up my loofah with tangerine exfoliating body wash and sanded my shoulders until the numbers *had* to be gone. My towel rubs a raw spot on the right side. A purple splotch blooming yellow at its edges. I dry water droplets off my forearms and brush a bruise in the shape of four fingers and a thumb, a patch of Velcro-scuffed skin, a blood blister, and the remnants of two large 1847s on both shoulders. What kind of marker *is* this? I grab a washcloth and soap the corner. Scrub again and manage to erase most of the 8 and 4 but the 1 and 7 on both arms stick. I hang the hand towel to dry, fold it to hide black Sharpie streaks on terrycloth. It's 5:30 and I need to be out of the house in twenty minutes. I'm not even dressed and the dinner starts at six. One last scrub at the residual ink and I drop the towel in the sink, tug my dress over my head.

The widow rings the doorbell as I'm curling my lashes. I slide across the hardwood in my stockings and open the front door. "Almost ready to go?" I turn and rush back into the bathroom and apply a double coat of mascara and make a final stop in the bedroom to grab my purse.

"What's the weather like?" I slip off my cardigan, move a piece of hair behind my ear, blend a bit of silver eye shadow, adjust my headband, untuck the floaty cap sleeve from my bra strap and follow the trail of bruises down both arms. 1, 8, part of a 7, skin flush against cool teal chiffon. The floors squeak as he paces the living room.

"Ready yet?" Cardigan back on, I squash my feet into shoes. High heels dig skate blisters. Kick them off. Flats.

* * *

Halfway through my eggplant parmesan, the back of my neck starts to sweat. I roll up both sleeves, slip my cardigan onto the chair-back. "Oh, I love the colour of your dress!" The woman next to me reaches out to touch the sleeve. "And the fabric! And—" She fumbles to grab her fork. Prods, stirs. Engages her food. I grab at my sleeve, my shoulder. The couple across from me hold eye contact with their pasta. Did I spill? Spit toothpaste in white splotches down my front? The widow leans his face to my ear over his wine glass: "your arms!" I snort. Grab a napkin and chuckle-cough into its folds. Scattered shoulder patches of purple, red and yellow.

"I'm not sure the bruises really match the dress, though." The widow busies himself with hasty mouthfuls of salad and pasta. "I had a roller derby bout last night. Got banged up a bit, but it was a really close game!" Sinister assumptions averted.

"Roller derby? What's that? That still exists? Here?" I may as well start at the beginning if I'm going to start somewhere and I've still got two more courses before dessert and coffee. I grab five creamers and five packets of butter and start arranging them on the table.

"Okay, so, this is what you call a pack…"

you want me to eat what?

"Does anyone here know how to eat the baby?"

Iva Sling's centre-track. 14 sets of eyebrows alert. *Eat what?*

"Eat the baby? Anyone?"

I catch Becky Check's eye and try to translate Iva's lesson. "Who understands team eat the baby?" I sign. Becky squints across the track at me.

"What?"

"Iva asked who understands team eat the baby?" My hand goes to my mouth in the sign for eat, and then mimics rocking a baby in my arms. Becky shakes her head.

"Eat the baby?" Becky signs. E-A-T B-A-B-Y, she fingerspells. Makes sure I know what I'm saying. 200 laps in 5 minutes all over again.

"Yes. Eat the baby." I point to Iva, centre-track explaining her modest proposal.

"When a jammer gets out of the pack with the other jammer on her heels, she can try to get her team to eat the baby."

I tap my head for jammer and gesture the proximity of the skaters. Then more "eat" and rocking an imaginary baby in my arms.

Iva pulls a group of skaters onto the track for a demo. The Black Team jammer breaks out of the pack with White's jammer right behind. The Black jammer slows down and holds her opponent back, while the Black Team blockers surround her and pull her back into the pack.

"See," says Iva. "Eat the baby."

"Ooooh, okay. Does that make sense?"

Becky nods. "Eat the baby," she signs. "I thought you were crazy."

Iva's moved on to lesson two. "Next, we're going to work on getting a goat."

"Now we're going to work on holding a, how do you sign G-O-A-T?"

"G-O-A-T?" Becky taps her fingers to her forehead for horns and a hand to her chin like a beard. "Goat."

post-practice thunder

I ate. I swear to Suzy Hotrod I ate before practice. I ate beans. And quinoa. And salsa. And green peppers. And tofu. I ate peanut butter and bananas. I ate cottage cheese. I ate blueberries. I ate cereal. I ate breakfast, lunch and dinner. I was full. Too full. I was convex and full of fuel for my three-hour practice.

Cut to 10 pm. Location: kitchen.

All cupboard doors swing open. The fridge looses cold air into the room. Crumb countertops. Jam smears. Drops of milk. A break-in. A loose dog. A rampaging bear. A sweat-stink derby girl rummaging in the freezer with one hand and sliding a sweaty sock off her foot with the other.

Must. eat. Must. eat. now. Must. eat. all. the. food.

Pour a bowl of cereal and milk. Almonds. Raisins. Scarf it down.

Rice cake with pb and j. Gone. Make another. Crumbs.

Pace the floor. Trace grout lines with one toe. What do I want to eat? Celery? Too much washing. Too much cutting. Need. Food. Now.

More cereal. More milk. Oatmeal. Crackers. Frozen berries. Last night's stir-fry. Cold. No time to microwave. Popcorn. More popcorn. Apple and peanut butter. Peanut butter banana. More berries. More cereal. Yogurt. Cottage cheese. More. More. Tortillas and hummus. Cheese and crackers. Smoothies. More cereal. Three bowls and two plates in the sink. Step ladder to the top shelf. There must be more food. Old Mother Hubbard went to the cupboard to fetch herself a seven-course post-practice snack.

Crunch. Chew. Swallow. Rumble. Rumble.

When she got there, the cupboard was bare, so she ordered a pizza.

achilles' heel

Horror film on late night TV. Scene one: a utility knife slashes a man's Achilles' tendons, blade through the backs of his ankles. My hairdryer deadens the shrieks. Scene two: sinking into my corduroy couch, feet laced tight inside shiny black skates. The leather heats around my feet, dryer three inches away. I press my heels back into the ankle support. Someone starts sawing at my Achilles'.

I almost hugged the mailman today when he rang the doorbell. I threw my phone onto the couch and sprinted for the door. CanadaPost online tracking: B.C., Mississauga, received at local post office, out for delivery. He hefted over the cardboard box, *thanks!* and I kicked the door closed behind me. Scissors. Keys. Something to slit the tape. I slid a ballpoint pen along the seam. *Rrippp*. Knee pads, gaskets, bearings, mouthguards, stoppers and stickers pile to one side to tote to practice. The team that orders gear together saves—*my skates!*

I tug the blue shoebox from the bottom of the shipping carton. Angels sing. Sun shines brighter through the windows. Clouds part. Tiny cartoon birds lift the lid.

They're sleek and black. Laces all the way to the toe. Clean leather speed boots with shiny axles and fresh nuts and washers. I rub my thumb along the sole stitching and dig in the side pocket of my derby bag for my skate tool. *Time to operate.* Cushions, stoppers, and wheels. Skate in my lap, axle rods digging red indents into thighs, I start in on the toe stoppers. Twist in a new set, nice and chunky. Fresh toe protectors to save the leather from scraping away with every trip. Unlace and re-lace both skates. Thick strips of blue duct tape over toe guards and bottom laces. *Friippp*. Skate between my knees, plate up, I start loosening the trucks. My old skates invade my nose as I drag them out of my bag and start unscrewing. Warehouse dust and dirt coats my fingers and the cushions as I pry them off and re-assemble them on the clean nylon plates, tighten up stoppers and bushings, just wheels to go. I spin my skate tool and loosen the axle nuts on my old skates, pop off the wheels, turn the boot in my hand, heel broken down, layers of duct tape shred over the toes. Blue. Silver. Black with skulls. Pink leopard print and blue mismatch laces. Toe protectors splitting. I transplant wheels onto fresh axles, bearings coated in grime. Last wheel still spinning, I grab my old skates and toss them onto the closet shelf. No wheels. No cushions. Naked boots ready to sell to any fresh zebras who show up. Spin old wheels *whiirrrr* on new skates. *Mmmm. Tonight's gonna be good.*

Crabby's geared up but benched, kneading the toe box of her boots with the heel of her palm. "Damn stupid skates. Gotta be the wrong size." She yanks off a slick sock and shows off black-purple toenails, polish-free. Her new skates arrived last week. I start to lace into mine, wiggling my toes to check for room. As I tug the laces tighter up my foot, I bite my lip. *What if they don't fit?*

Onto the track and, *shit shit shit!* my trucks slip out of control. My right foot wants to slide out at the front and the left is like skating on a squirrel. I wobble back to my bag, grab a skate tool and start adjusting. Attempt number two and the trucks still aren't right but my ankles—heel box gnashes my Achilles'. I stop and Becky Check catches my grimace. Plowing out through the heels means pushing my ankle into the back of the skate. Another quarter truck turn and the squirrels are gone but the trench in my ankle digs deeper. Becky's suggesting leather oil and Lily Bad thinks heat setting the boot might help but for now all I've got is my foot to work in the heel. Breathe. Out. Breathe. Out. I round the track, leather etching flesh round the bends. Jump. Transition. Run down the straight-aways. Jammer start. *ahhhhh!* Angling my feet and running on my toes grates ankle-flesh against the heel box. I should have sent the mailman back. Two hours of cringing laps and I'm done. New skates: 2. Pain Eyre: 0. I pull the laces loose and slip out, ankles rejoicing.

On the couch, hairdryer and stir-fry in hand, I fork rice and veggies into my mouth and blow-dry boots at once. I press my ankles back into the leather and tendons yelp. My phone chirps.

"How're the new skates?" I click off the dryer to text back.

"Great." I grab my skate tool and start spinning off the wheels. The horror movie wails, shrieks. I hit mute and open the closet to grab my old crumbling skates. Ripped toe guard. Mismatch tape. Grubby laces. I thumb the beat-up heel box. Maybe just one more practice, for old times' sake. Maybe just a few more practices.

greta grip

When Greta Grip hit the Sin Bin she hit hard.

Greta always hits hard, hips checking jammers to the ground when they try to sneak around her on the inside line. Green pivot behind her, Greta Grip in blue swings her hips, keeps Green back but trips. Green clips her skate and goes down behind— *BLUE NUMBER ONE low blocking major!*

Third trip to the Sin Bin and only two minutes to play, down fourteen points in the final tournament game. Greta swings around the outside track, plows in front of Sin Bin seats. Takes a knee, wrist guards slam down on plastic. *Crack!*

Greta took out the girl with her hips, then her wheels, got sent to the box.

Took out the box.

Fists hover out in front like the chair still stands. Metal legs and plastic seat in a heap.

Penalty time starts when a skater sits in the penalty seat.

Greta grabs for the next Sin Bin chair, sits. Toe-stops the rubble to her right. Snapped seat clatters legs, scrapes concrete. Timer beeps.

bout day

Woke up thirsty, with last night's omelet at the back of my throat. Must be bout day. I fill my litre-and-a-half bottle up past the brim and start sipping. Bathroom. Sip. Living room. Sip. Sip. Laundry room. Sip. Kitchen. Sip.

> Pain Eyre's bout day breakfast:
> 1/2 cup (measured uncooked) stove-top quick oats
> Mix in:
> one apple (chopped and heated in the microwave)
> handful of raw almonds
> handful of raisins
> teaspoon of brown sugar
> a couple shakes of cinnamon
> a slurp of almond milk.

I dump the thick mix into a bowl and carry it steaming to the couch, singeing fingers on ceramic. Sip. Boot up my laptop. Search: bout footage, today's opponents. Damn, nothing recent. Search: "knee starts roller derby." No videos. "Scrum starts roller derby." No videos. "World Cup Roller Derby." Results: Canada versus U.S.A. The final. My voice fizzled screaming for Team Canada during that game. I shovel oatmeal into my mouth between gulps of water. Pause. Unpause. Replay the start of each jam. What are the jammers doing? Lateral steps looking for a hole through the scrum? Pushing forward with a shoulder? Who gets out first? Pause. Unpause. Pause. Unpause. It's too fast to watch it straight through. Jammers running on the spot. See a hole. Go for it. Hole closes. Get hit. Try again. My stomach gurgles. Oatmeal rising in my throat.

Pain Eyre's bout day to-do list:

    Sip.

    Sip.

    Sip.

    Pack derby gear bag: Knee pads, elbow pads, gaskets, wrist guards, helmet, skates, back up wheels, skate tool, mouthguard, back up mouthguard.

    Shower.

    Change clothes: Cotton underwear. Compression pants. Black skirt. Sports bra. Jersey. Make-up pads and duct tape for ankle bite. Sports socks. Leg warmers. Track jacket.

    More clothes for the gear bag: extra socks. Extra skirt. Snot rag.

    Deodorant.

    Hit the fridge. Two bottles of reduced sugar sports drink.

    Check gear bag again.

    Again.

An hour until I have to leave and my eyes are drained from pause-unpause squinting at starts. Time to clean the bathroom. Wipe down surfaces. Mop the floor. Me on the jammer line against a scrum start opposing team. Where do I go? Put one shoulder forward and run on my stoppers. Laterals to find a hole. Their jammer's still trapped but not for long. Flush the toilet. Wipe down the walls of the shower. See a hole in the pack. Explode through it. She's out first. Catch her at turn three, force her to call it off. 0 - 0 jam. What time is it? Fifteen minutes before I have to hit the venue. Lunch.

Doorbell.

One second Crabby! Keys. Phone. Wallet. Kick-slam the door behind me.

"Where's your gear bag?" Shit. My stomach gurgles again. Water. Omelet. Oatmeal. Bout day breakfast climbing back up my throat.

derby deeds

Delivery truck driver. Used car sales receptionist. Medical transcriptionist. Five plus years experience. College certification. Forklift operation license. Industrial painting experience. Scroll down. Next page. Scroll down. Eyes droop. Where's the lamp and when did it get so dark? 10:45? I've been scrolling jobs for over two hours. I can type. Sure. I can proofread. But I don't have a dental receptionist job in my history, or in my future apparently. I can communicate, sure. Last night, the coach called me out on not communicating enough during a pack drill. *Why don't I hear the pivot?* The pivot. Oh shit, that's me. Pivot panty on my helmet I started yelling, *outside! Inside! Jammer coming up! Behind Greta!* Communication skills, check. Shorthand experience? No. Next job. Assembly experience? I can disassemble, clean, and reassemble bearings, bushings, and trucks no problem. I can tell you the right durometer of wheels for a slippery floor or sticky hardwood. I can spout details about alloy cores, hybrid urethanes, and 62s versus 59s when it comes to acceleration. Physiotherapist's assistant? No training, but I can feel when a quad is pulled or a hamstring's too tight. Personal trainer? Un-certified. But I can do burpees on skates, squat for three hours, and get a tired team moving *go go go just a few more laps ladies, finish strong!*

Pain Eyre has a full-time volunteer derby career. So why can't derby be my job? Wake up in the morning and get paid to tweet about the latest wheels I tested. Chug a new protein shake before practice and blog about the effects. Research stretches for lower back strain. Email off a press kit to an emerging league. Proof an article on the no-minors rules set. Wake up. Derby. Lunch. Derby. Practice. Fall asleep watching bouts online.

Job search: roller derby. One result. I blink twice and click the link. Roller derby magazine editor? Roller derby promotions manager? Roller derby fitness blogger?

Steam roller operator: Derby, UK.

northern line

Three full practices? I am going to miss three full practices. Eight hours of skate time. How many minutes is that? Eight times 60. 480 minutes, give or take water breaks, depending on the heat. Let's say 420 minutes total. 25,200 seconds off-skates while my team will be on-skates. Nine full days without a moment laced into my quads. I haven't been nine days off-skates in two years. When I pulled a hip-flexor, I took off two practices and showed up in sneakers to learn the drills. When I tore a quad, I skipped one. I threw my lower back doing push-ups and crawled to the chiropractor so I could lace up next practice.

Nine whole days with my skates 3762 miles away. I can't even strap them on for a roll in the park or a living room side-step agility workout. Nine days and my skates won't recognize my feet anymore. Nine hours on a plane to lose muscle tone and memory. Planking in the aisles might trip up flight attendants. Squats in the bathroom will lead to a line.

Derby leagues crop up in every city in my travel plans. Can I tack on a practice as a visiting skater? I fire off emails to three leagues for details. When, where, how much and do you have gear? My gear bag would eat a baggage allowance on its own. Nine whole days. Just one practice? A day of touristing, a quick change into some derby garb, hop three buses and the tube to the other side of town for a scrimmage.

Except,

practice times criss-cross travel. I'm training and busing while they're training and juking.

Or,

"No gear to lend. Sorry." No bouts to watch. No strategy to snag. No commemorative t-shirt to bring back. Nine days completely derby free.

Except.

I'll gain hip advantage in the tube station and booty block my way onto the train. Crowd compressing toward the door, one leg in front of the woman to my right. Shift into her position. Sideways through the businessmen on my left. Hip lean train-door standers to squeeze off the platform (mind the gap). Duck under arms and slip past *doors closing. Please keep all items away from closing doors.* No seats. Train jolt and stumble. Derby stable stance.

Or,

Three-wall up front. Moving side by side, no gaps. They're not looking back. Find a hole, wait for them to stagger. Pick out the weakest point and strike. The girl on the right takes a turn slightly slower, opens up a small space. Shoot forward to slip through the gap sideways. Shopping bags graze my thighs. My purse tangles on her handbag. *Sorry, excuse me* and dart through passengers meandering to their connecting train.

Or,

Wall-up on Piccadilly crosswalks and compress around street corners. *Pack is here!* to stay together in the throngs and *Out of play!* to re-form our pack. *Touch two!* push travel teammates into walls to hold our place in castle and tower queues. Derby stance over public toilets.

Or,

Jam the crowds in Oxford Street. Slipping in between shoppers multi-player blocking with their Harrods bags. Move your feet on the escalator. Four floors of five-dollar shirts, ten-dollar dresses, hundreds of shoppers excavating deals in racks and bins, baby buggies and shopping baskets in tow. Pace line through the accessories, weave around the swimsuit section, jump a pile of hangers on the floor, and *pack is back!* reverse back to release a goat, blocked in behind an arguing couple. Avoid a back block and speed through the men's section dodging women holding shirts to boyfriends' chests, kids tugging at jeans pockets and workers hanging and re-hanging pants. Clear line to the checkout. Race alongside a shopper with the same idea, sidestep through racks, throw a hip, hop a handbag, break a wall and three big steps *will this be everything today?*

Nine days. Completely. Derby. Free.

no sorry in derby

"Guys. Guys, I'b bleedin. By bouth ib bleedin." Iva hockey stops at the edge of the track as I lift my hands away from my face.

"Oh no, not again Pain!" Blood mingles with floor-dust. I spit out my mouthguard, red smudge. "Here, I'll wash it. You go with first aid." I move to pass her my used-to-be-white-before-we-skated-in-a-dirty-warehouse mouthguard, greying in the teeth-prints with flecks of red. I pull back my hand.

"I got it Iba. Don't bant you to hab to touch thab." I roll into the hall, hand over face, blood drying between my fingers. Iva holds back my helmet straps as I rinse off my mouth at the fountain. I run my tongue across the inside of my upper lip. Skin-gap, split down the centre. Cold water bites and rinses red down the steel reservoir.

Lily Bad unwraps a 4x4 gauze. "Hold it down for a few minutes, and wet it before you pull it off or else half your lip is coming with it." Nod and remember peeling cloth out of my thigh last summer. Grab the gauze and press.

At water break, Greta Grip skates over from the track. "God Pain, I'm so sorry." *There's no sorry in derby.* The phrase we trot out every time a check sends us flying into the brick wall, or our fall trips up the eight skaters behind us in the pace line. The phrase I parrot every time I get smacked in the face.

"No wobbies! No sobby in duhby, bight?" I roll back to centre-track to mumble scrum strategy through cotton.

"Again Pain, really?"

"Is it your nose?"

"What happened to your face?"

A whistle *screeeeees*. I grab for the mouthguard in my skirt pocket, slam plastic against gauze. Oh yeah. "Pain, might want to sit this one out." Split lips sink ships.

ode to old knee pads

Dear knee pads,

When I first picked you up, I admit, you were attached. But you'd lived your whole life on the shelf. I could see a future for us. You undid me, and I just had to undo you. When I felt the warmth of you wrapped around me for the first time, I swore from then on we'd never be apart.

New pads, fresh skates, glinting shiny black in the sun of our first practice space. I picture you as you were then: un-marked. Un-scathed. Fresh, like my knees, elbows and arms that first August, now so scratched and bruised.

When coach yelled *fall!* I stumbled. I didn't want to hurt you. We'd only just got together. But I fell. For you and on you. Mostly when I didn't want to. I was a baby giraffe on skates, all flailing limbs and tumbles. And you protected me. Against torn skin and contusions. Softened blows and concrete kisses. You got into scrapes for me, and it began to show. Scratches, scuffs.

And you started to smell. I stood with you. I needed you. Two months in, still stumbles and slow, other skaters were starting to stare. To avoid us on the track. Your cheese and vinegar aura pushed them away, so I ran a bath for you. Steamed up the room with hot water and soap and gave you time to soak, relax. You deserved the break after all you'd done for me. I brought you out on the porch to dry off a little, to sun bathe. Still damp, and clinging to that familiar scent, you joined me at practice the next day. But this time, I stood up for you. It was *our* moldy cheese. *Our* kitty litter. We were in this together.

Over the next few months, we started to grow apart. You drifted away and I had to pull tight to hang onto you. You were distant, but you still kept me safe. I tore my upper leg on the concrete, and scratched my shoulder on a wall, but my knees stayed strong. We single knee fell, double knee fell, did small falls and falls we didn't mean to do. You helped me baseball fall, run suicide drills, picking up scuffs and scratches for me every time.

When we started scrimmaging I realized how much you did for me. Wheels locked. Hits connected. Jumps failed, but you were always there to make the save. One night, I left you behind, thinking I didn't need you for a quick skate around the park. I spilled without you and I never missed you so much. My knee purpled, grew, and refused to bend and I finally understood how much I relied on you this one time that you weren't there. After that, you grew distant, less helpful. I dropped down for a knee fall and nerves twinged. Tripped up in a scrimmage and asked for ice, my knee burning from the inside out. I had worn you down, and it was starting to show.

Icing a swollen joint one night, I laid you out on the floor. Counted twenty four scratches, your straps twisted. You were in bad shape, but after what we had been through, I couldn't part with you. I know you never forgave me for the night I left you behind. One practice, mid-way through the season, I tripped in a pace line and felt that pang. My knee heating up, growing angry. I thought you may have slipped, but no. Your cap had pulled away from cloth, plastic dangling. You were hurt and I could only offer a band-aid. Four strips of duct tape and I told myself you were fine, you'd pull through. But with each practice, each skid began to purple my knees more and more. You were on your way out, we were over, and I knew it. I just wasn't ready to admit it yet. I wasn't ready to move on.

We road-tripped to a speed skating class, and no surprise, I tripped over my own feet. Crashed down onto hard wood. Sticky. No slide. I limped up and felt heat rising in my knee. On the way home, we stopped at a skate shop, shiny new knee pads, plastic caps in pink, red, purple, and black. A pair caught my eye. They looked like you when we first got together and I admit I took them home that night. I wrapped them around me and felt the difference, how exhausted you had become without me noticing. I needed to end things, to move on to something new or else we'd both just keep getting hurt. I hoped you would understand.

I brought the new pads to practice the next day, but I kept you around. What if I needed you? What if they didn't work out? What if we weren't a good fit? With them I did everything I wished I could still do with you. I fell without hesitation, rock star slid across the concrete and felt no pain. But I didn't forget about you. Knee pads, you were still with me, and on my mind, and today I took you out. I ran you a bath and helped you freshen up, to look your best. I trimmed your duct tape bandages, blue and silver. Straightened your straps. Dusted your caps off.

I hope you understand how much I learned during our time together. It's not your fault I wore you out, and I'm sorry things have to end this way. But you'll find someone new. A visiting skater or fresh meat. Someone who treats you better than I did. Who appreciates you more and won't slip up so much.

I'm truly sorry I hurt you. I didn't mean to fall so hard.

Thank you knee pads. Thank you from the bottom of my thighs.

playing chicken

Black shirts to the rotisserie!

Footfalls pound the parking lot. A pause for the automatic doors and we scramble inside the grocery store. *This way!* Iva Sling and Becky Check dart down one aisle with Crabby Apple steps behind. Becky steps out into Crabby's path. Throws a hip check that nearly sends her careening into the granola bars and rice cakes. Walls up with Iva to keep Crabby behind. Shoes basketball squeak on tile.

A cashier takes slow strides. Stands at the end of the aisle, hands on hips, frown lines deepening. Iva stops blocking, stands up straight out of derby stance and turns to the shelves. She grabs a jar of jam and *hmmms* and *aahs* the nutritional content. Becky and Crabby snap to standing, stroll the aisle and nod to the cashier. She snorts and turns back to her checkout.

Pack is here! I shout over jars of pickles and cans of soup on skids blocking the aisle. Midnight re-stocking staff on break. Iva's found her target, locked in, and is running toward the hot foods section. *I'm bridging, I'm bridging!* Arms out in both directions, I occupy the space between Iva, Becky and Crabby, as they sprint forward to re-form the pack. *Pack is all!* Game over. The prize? The last two rotisserie chickens at the grocery store. Post bout cravings. With a box of oatmeal under one arm, I follow my teammates to the checkout, panting from the second evening exertion. *Will that be everything?* Chicken. Oatmeal. Sweat, poultry and maple sugar. Let's get this after-party started.

shiner

A split lip. A bloody nose. A goose egg. An elbow to the ear. Marker smears under the chin. Numbers smudge from arms to cheeks. I've been hit in the face more times than I can count on my wheels. I've tracked bruises tie-dying knees, butt, arms, legs, hips. Black and purple, fading to yellow and green. Bruises I don't remember receiving. Bruises that pang every time flesh meets chair. But never a black eye.

I gave Greta the first shiner of the season. Punched her in the eye and skated on. Fist met face and I felt nothing. 45 minutes after the bout, after I dried my hair under the hand dryer in the change room, switched into fresh socks, and zipped my wet gear into its bag, I passed her in the parking lot on the way to the after-party. "Oh my god your eye!" A raised welt and a line of purple deepening just above her cheek.

In the pack: I'm jamming, fighting hard through a wall of green shirts. See a gap and sprint forward. Don't look back.

How could I not have noticed? Ten skaters in the pack, hits left right and left again, skates to hop, grabbing whips and pushing through walls. How could I have noticed?

My phone chirps. Greta posted a new photograph. Purple streak growing darker. A real shiner. Chirp. Chirp. Chirp. Chirp. Comments rattle my phone.

> Beautiful!
> Amazing!
> I love it!
> So sexy!
> Looking good!

My turn: I am so so so so sorry.

A shiny purple battle badge.
A bout night souvenir.
No sorries in derby. She only wishes it were darker.

go ahead and jump!

Watching myself skate on camera is like hearing my voice on the radio. Do I really say *um* and *like,* like, that often and is my voice *that* scratchy? That high-pitched? Do I really skate *that* slowly, and are my arms *quite* that prone to flailing in the middle of the pack? My news feed warned that video from Saturday's bout had emerged onto the internet. I snagged a bag of baby carrots and a Tupperware of hummus to munch, face pressed close to my laptop screen, pausing, un-pausing and re-pausing. Skating too tall behind that four wall. Should have thrown a hit on that jammer instead of trying to maneuver in front of her. Move your feet *come on move your feet!* Juke, jump, do something. Don't look so *tired* all the time. Get up faster!

I track the sources of my bruises, piecing together hits, misses, trips and slides into a map of black, blue, and yellowing skin. The other jammer slides across the floor, kicks a foot up into my ankle. Picks up a low block, major. I earn a green tender stripe across the shin. A couple jams later, I grab the hips of the blocker in front and swing into the opposing jammer. An education in what works. And what doesn't.

Watching myself attempt to jump the apex on film? That's like listening to my own voice recorded. Drunk. On my ex's answering machine. The scratchy high-pitchedness is the least cause of my burning cheeks. Jumping the apex is like performing one of those backwards-over-your-head bicycle kicks in soccer. Do it correctly, with the right timing and connect with the ball. It sails past the goalkeeper into the back of the net. A second off one way or the other? Connect with nothing. Fly backwards into the air, leg over head, and slam spine into grass.

An apex jump: see the opportunity, take the step, leap off one foot and try to land it effortlessly on the other side, slipping past multiple blockers while airborne without cutting the track. It can be beautiful. It can inspire gasps from the audience, cheers from your bench, instant replays, and knowing nods from the opposing team who can respect the awesome-ness that is your apex jump.

It's a Suzy Hotrod move. A Bonnie Thunders move. An Iron Wench move. And in the video clip currently rolling, it's about to become a Pain Eyre move. Except I'd already rubbed the bruises on both knees. I'd seen the photographs, skates in the air, and then knees on the ground. But I had never seen it in action. On film. Until now, the videographer kindly slowing the moment down for maximum impact.

Two minutes into the clip, I take what felt like a giant forward leap off one foot, but on film is just a slight hop. Still, I'm up, off my skates and *bam!* Yellow number 35 slams into my side, with her teammate right next to her, ready to take another hit. My legs fly up and the cement floor approaches. Knees slam against the concrete as the blocker hits the floor behind me with the force of her hit. I can't see the zebra's fingers, but there's a chance I snagged those two points. My jump's about as pretty as my knees and it hardly deserves a slow-motion replay, but I can't help but pause un-pause pause re-pause my apex jump failure: back to the start.

jam stopper

TOE STOPPER! rolls across the track into the ref lane. *Inside!* I shove Lily hard, plow to hold centre-track. *Umph!* She connects with the jammer, hip checks over the line. Tomahawks and runs back. *SOMEBODY! TOE STOPPER!* The head ref holds the stopper stem high above the pack. *STOPPER LOOSE!* Jammer approaching on the outside, I shuffle to wall up with Greta. White shirt pushing hard on our backs, our jammer whips off Greta on the inside and ducks through the pack. *Mary Kate Smashley picks up leeaaaad jammer!* The inside pack ref scans the cluster of skates shuffling left, right, hockey stop, step, step hit, for a missing stopper. White jammer up on her toes, darts outside and breaks past our wall. I cut the angle straight for her and connect hard, skate backwards into the fast pack. *She's out! Wall up!* Half a minute ticks and no claims on the stopper. The pack stampede shuffles, White throwing hits on our wall to open jammer-sized holes. *Pain!* A man's voice. Eyes centre-track to follow the sound. *Oomph!* Shoulder: crunch ribs. *PAIN! It's yours! THE STOPPER!* The zebra skates centre-track, pointing down at my foot like it's lead jammer. Eight feet jostling. Stripes. Socks. Pink. Blue. Black laces. Bump wheels. My right toe guard flaps open. No stopper. *Jammer, outside!* White jammer's back. Gotta find my wall. Just don't put down that toe. A cement face plant. A skate to the nose. A somersault through the pack. The White jammer slips past on my outside, four whistles, Smashley slamming hands to hips to call it off. Backwards transition, and—no stopper. Skate boots mid-tilt. Don't put down that toe. I hockey stop to collect my missing hardware. My skate tool's back on the bench. Stride, stride, turnaround, stoppers—

Ooooh shit! Tip forward and over front wheels. A missing stair. A trip-wire.
Clatter clatter concrete.

I told you not to put down that stopper.

day off

Canada Day practice: cancelled. Watch fireworks and eat a hamburger. Wave paper flags. Sparkler-burn fingers. Horseshoes and corncobs. Relatives and derby widows. Red and white streamers. Derby-free day.

I toss a pair of old gaskets, a worn-out skate bag, and two hand weights out of a cardboard box. Eight outdoor wheels bounce and roll across the hardwood. I dive onto my kneepads, clutch after the one disappearing under the couch and wipe the cobwebs off my shirt. Sweat pools in arm-crooks and saturates my elbow pads. 40 minutes to get downtown.

I dig in my skate bag for a tool, slipping wheels on axles and tightening nuts pit-stop quick. Helmet on, buckle undone, wristguards in hand, I trip out the front door and onto the porch. My left lace frays, its threads locked in Velcro teeth, pink leopard print shredding on porch steps. I tuck in the loose fibres and move on to the right. Toes laced separately, skip a hole, second set of laces. Tight but not numb. Tug pink laces taught and—SNAP.

30 minutes to get downtown. Enough lace left to adjust, pull through eyelets evenly and knot. Velcro strap, helmet snap. Let's go. Porch step. Step. I toe-stopper step down onto the cracked pavement, weeds and rocks on asphalt. It's no smooth slick concrete track. I stumble step onto the road and the vibrations reach my knees. Pushing hard against the street, rocks catch underfoot, wheels spitting them out the sides of skates. 26 minutes to get downtown. My toes tingle from the whirring by the time I plow at the corner. Car. Car. Car. Van. Gap.

Drivers giraffe at the girl in full gear, not your average summer blader. I cringe down the bike lane, too narrow for wide strides, with cars whipping by on my outside. Car. Van. Van. Gap. Cross the street and down the ramp to the path, legs plowing wide to check my speed. Whipping down the slope, my hands shake, wide-eyes for rocks and wood chips: downhill booby traps.

15 minutes to get downtown through the bicycle and jogger avoidance course. Clipping down the path, I hop puddles and patches of gravel. Tiny hops, one foot to the other, then two-foot jump the patch of flowerbed spill cedar chips. Dodge an e-bike or two, slip past a couple strolling hand-in-hand down the bike lane. Now, three minutes left to get back to the street. A ramp: interlocking brick. The gaps in the brickwork jolt my calves and catch my wheels; stoppers clipping raised edges send me stumbling. Bricks: 3. Pain: 0. Wide stance, I duck walk the rest of the ramp, jump on the sidewalk, and cruise into the parking lot.

Canada Day: a well-deserved derby break. Seven skaters dump backpacks and handbags in trunks of cars. *Is that everyone? Let's go!* Back down the sidewalk toward the path. Six in knee pads and me in full-gear. Sweat slips down helmet pads, tickles my ears and neck.

"You've got your helmet on in this heat?" Shrug. *When do I ever fall on my elbows* bloodied both arms last summer, jumping storm debris by the river in front of carnival-goers and picnic gawkers. This year, I'm not taking chances.

We cross the street, seven skaters plus three on long boards and search for the best way down to the path. Ramp, grass or stairs? I follow Smashley and Becky down the stairs, railing-clutch, toe-stopper step. Back on the pathway, it's time to jam. One-by-one we weave through the carnival, hop cables powering the Tilt-a-Whirl and duck shooting games. *What the hell do you think you're doing?* Five more skaters pass in front of the strength-test booth shouts. No time for cotton candy or a corn dog. The breeze kicks off the river and airs the sweat off my back. Skating into the wind pushes hard against my legs and my head drip drips. I snag a water-bottle swig, un-strap my helmet and tug it off, mussing hair with my fingers and detaching wet strands from my forehead. I catch Smash and Greta, hear the rumble of wheels and bearings behind. Six pack it up along the path. *Touch two!* Wall up. Keep your teammates in arms' reach. Rest hands on thighs, smalls of backs. Pack instinct.

dance off

Right. Now front. Back. Turn. No wait, is it front or back first? Shit. Greta and I crossover, tap. Step forward. Tap. Step back. Tap. Turn and crossover again. *Doo doo doo doo doodoo doo doo doo. Do the hustle!*

Votes on scrap paper. Travel team tie-breaker. "Does anyone have a pen?"

Blue lines. Red lines. Gym mats and Velcro walls. Time-out in the corner to wait out the vote. Step back. Tap. Turn. Crossover. Greta vs. Pain for assistant-captain. I gnaw my inside lip. Pens scratch.

"We'll settle this on the dance floor instead." Crossover. Forward. Back. Turn. Toe-stopper steps. Footwork workout. Greta slips and laughs as she pulls herself up off the dusty rubber floor. Last one standing, queen of the rink. *Does that mean I win?*

Crabby's shuffling scraps, counting votes while Lily waits centre-track, stretching quads and calves. She picked up enough votes for captain, but the assistant spot tied. Tied, despite my clear toe-stop-hustle prowess.

What did I even say? Um, it's been over a year on skates. I'd like to motivate the team. Errr, push an extra lap out of us all. I, uh, love derby. We all say that, we all love derby. But I really do. It's my life. I guess it's all of our lives. Um… I'm confident appealing bad calls, I guess. I'll um, keep reading the rules. Uh…Why couldn't I get it out? Words for why I skate, why I know I'd be good for the C. I should have mentioned listening. Team communication. Bouting goals. Rankings. Too late. She crumples the votes in one hand.

"It's a tie again! Greta and Pain, jammer line. Race!"
Seriously? I push off toward the track but Crabby calls me back. "Kidding!" I flip my skate

up on its back axle. Tap front wheels on the rubber floor. Crabby holds a scrap note in one hand, folded in half. She opens it like an Oscar envelope and demands a drum roll of clicking wheels and stomping skates. My stomach flops and starts creeping up my throat.

"Welcome your travel team captains ladies…May they lead you on to many victories!" Tap tap tap. Skate on rubber. Come on Crabby—

"Lily Bad aaaaaaand…"

I ball up my face, squint my eyes almost closed, and suck sharp air through mouthguard plastic.

"Aaaaand…Pain!"

What?

SCREEEEE!

Coach Ryan Ginger whistles to call us all into centre-track. Hugs and hip-checks. Playbooks and pens. "Our next game is in less than three weeks. Let's get strategizing. Pain, Lily? Any ideas?"

Lips chap. Stomach flips. Back walls, front walls. Goats. Slow. Fast. Knee starts. Need. Water. "Um, errrr, I…I think…"

"Wait, did everyone hand in their shirt sizes yet?"

Gulp. Chew a hole through my lip. Pen tapping on my playbook. Only three weeks. New jerseys on order. Back walls, front walls. Bulls and goats. Scrum starts. Slow starts. Spreadsheet size, name and number.

Pain Eyre, 1847. Medium shirt. Small shorts.

An asterisk in pen next to Lily's name. And mine.

Can't forget the letter C.

spartans

Half-time: we're down by 15, and losing fire fast. I tear open a protein bar and roll into the suicide seating, gnawing off hunks of chocolate mint. Sweat wanders down my back and pools on the waistband of my tights. My arms collect traces of other people's numbers. A couple letter Ls. Half an 8. 1, 4 and 7 smudged off.

The widow stands up from his spot track-side, brandishing a Bristol board, I HEART PAIN in giant capital letters. I grin and slide off my helmet. Run fingers through soaking hair, un-matting tangles from my head. "Their jammers are just getting through so quickly. I can't get lead if they slip through like that." I shake my head out, sweat flying off to the sides like a dog after rain. "I need to pick up more points."

"Listen." He holds up the other side of the sign. BRING ON THE PAIN. "Listen. You're skating hard. Just keep pushing. They'll get tired. You've got more energy."

I slide into the bench gasping from each jam, dry air from the floor rosin caking my throat. Cough cough splutter. Choke down half a bottle of sports drink without taking a breath. I don't feel like I have more energy.

A buzzer sounds. Five minutes to the second-half and I still need to wipe down my arms and re-number.

"PAIN!"

"Yeah?"

"Remember, come back with your shield or on it."

With my shield or on it. Dead or victorious. Be a Spartan on the track. Give it all or give nothing. Shields up. Shoulder to shoulder. No holes! Got it. *For Spartans, war was respite from their impossibly difficult training for war.* I came back on my shield.

bearing bath

A blonde hair uncoils from around and around around around an axle. I let it loose into the breeze and nudge the stack of eight wheels on the porch, rag-wiping dusty trucks, axles, and boot, crud collecting in cloth creases. Warehouse dust slips into crevices Monday/Thursday. My bearings cake, whirr and slow spin.

Grease smudges my thigh skin and the hems of my shorts. Red indents and axle grooves in my leg, I drop my skate tool with a clank on the concrete. Creak stiff bearings out.

I slide a loose wheel back on an axle, rock it back and forth, catch threading into the bearing and pry. Pry. Slip. Try again. Wiggle back and forth and forth back. A creak. Looser. And then—pop. A dark bearing, once silver and red, slides down the axle. I turn it in my fingers, safety pin pop off the cover and plop both into an old cream cheese tub. Rubbing alcohol pulls at the grime, red peeking through brown. Chunks and specks drift in clear liquid, then float to the bottom. Next bearing.

Pry, pry and slip again. An axle catches skin and slices thin down my finger. *Fffff*—.

Grease on my hands, the cut bites and bites again when I drop the next bearings in the tub. A splash and a burn.

Another bearing, another. Eight from each skate clattering together in the plastic. Hair sliding from between metal rings, liquid dying grey then brown.

Ethyl burns my skin, plucking rings from their bath. The sun sucks up the damp and dries the grey patches on the porch as I dump months of warehouse dust, hair and stick from skate nights at the bar, sugar water track, rosin powder, bathroom floor pick-up: bearing bath water. Dump it all out the tub. Skate brew. Grass killer.

16 shiny bearings and clean red caps in a row across the porch.
Eight wheels in a stack.
Two clean skates. Dirt still stows in the stitches. Clean*er*.
And one skate tool to put the whole thing back together again.

45 minutes until practice. Fingers fly over bearings dripping speed cream, spinning. Re-clipping covers. 45 minutes until wheels re-start their collection. Gum. Soil. Dead skin. Glitter. Cake dust over shiny red and silver rings. Collect and coil stray hairs. Around and around around around.

price on my head

Cooking eggs over easy in the kitchen, a chinstrap grazes my shoulder. Checking emails in the living room, I catch earflaps in my peripheral vision. My derby helmet airs out on the porch with the rest of my gear, de-sweating but not de-stinking from last night's practice. I scarf down a bowl of cinnamon-sprinkled popcorn and flick through bad afternoon television. *Ten top tips for boosting your metabolism after the break.* What apartment hazards require a hockey helmet?

* * *

"One hundred and thirty dollars? Is that how much they cost?" The clerk at the sports store holds out a black helmet for me to try on and shows me how to adjust the fit. I snug the helmet onto my head and feel…compressed.

"It's going to feel tight, a lot tighter than a skateboard helmet." My derby helmet boasts layers of stickers and more stickers, the padding inside washed, re-washed and worn down from almost two years of two-practice-a-week wear. I slip it on before my skates and back off again to air out my head on a water break, ventilation holes sealed over with skate shop logos and promos for other leagues. Round and smooth. Scuffs.

I run my hands over the lumpy jammer panty un-friendly plastic. Elastic edges won't slip smooth over these juts and bumps. I adjust the strap and catch my palm on the earflaps. No more stray fists or elbows to the ear.

"Is this really *that* much better than the lower end model?" The clerk nods and rattles off names of hockey players. Somebody Wellwood. Carcillo. Sidney who? Fighters and skill-players. The model they use. "Never heard of them."

"Shall I ring you through at the check-out then?"

My head smacks the cement floor, brain careening from the front of my skull to the back. Cartoon shock waves surge through my cortex.

I tug on the chinstrap. Snug. How many skulls can you buy for a hundred and thirty dollars?

I pull the helmet off and run a hand through my hair, over my scalp. No splits. No stitches. No concussions, yet. I pull out my credit card.

This is your brain on roller derby.

take a knee

Four medics snap blue surgical gloves at the wrists. A flash of orange behind navy uniforms. God, is that a backboard? Blue wheels spinning, spinning, slow, stop. The bottom of one knee pad. I clack clack across the concrete track on my knees to catch a better vantage point. The crowd arc their necks from suicide seating and whisper to one another. *Is she okay?* They open bout programs to rosters. *Which one is it? The tiny one.* The medics wall in the skater, flat on the track. Shuffling. Adjusting her legs. No blood. No visible bone. Two lift all hundred pounds of skater, skates and pads onto an orange board with straps. Wheels squeak over the hush. No sponsorship ads or music. Just a stretcher arriving through the Zamboni door.

Skaters, return to your benches.

The pack, kneeling, foot-tapping and lip biting, stand and coast back to their seats, throw down water as Mary Kate Smashley, back board, skates and knee pads meets stretcher. Blue gloves cover her legs with a blanket, wheels and skate laces jutting out the bottom. A zebra slips the jammer panty off Smashley's helmet and skates it over to our bench. With a thumbs up to the zebra crew, the stretcher moves toward the waiting ambulance.

SMASHLEY! SMASHLEY! SMASHLEY! SMASHLEY!

Our bench, voices cracking from 45 minutes of *inside! outside! offense! goat, now!* raises the chant. SMASHLEY! SMASHLEY! SMASHLEY! Wheels stomp the concrete as the other bench joins in. Then the crowd on the floor. The crowd in the stands. Stomping the risers and clapping hands.

The stretcher turns the corner out the arena door and it's *two minutes to warm back up.* Up off knees and seats. Back onto the track. Bench coach tosses me the jammer panty. *Let's win this for Smashley!* One jammer down, and 35 points to make up in fifteen minutes. I tug the panty over my helmet, toe-stopper the jammer line and wait for the whistles.

*   *   *

Fifteen minutes later we're centre track posing for photos. Flashes and camera phones. *Just one more shot!* Lily Bad's clutching flowers in one hand and her helmet in the other, captain's C sweat-smearing down her arm. *One more, one more!* Smile. Pose. Flash. Flash. Shutter. Click. Twenty feet away, the other team lifts the trophy. Smile. Pose. Flash. Shutter. Click.

Hockey helmet under one arm, Smashley steps into the arena. "Need any help with the tape?" Stretcher, ambulance, ER. X-rays instead of team snapshots.

"Sorry we couldn't win it for you." Our second place photo finish deserves a cheer. *We're number two!*

Time to take another knee. Peel up the track. End of a season. Skates and helmets off, hair lank and wet, we knee pad clatter across the floor, scratching at tape and rope. Tug. Collecting stray programs from the empty stands. Black shirts and blue, ripping the last scraps of derby off the floor.

snapshot

A photograph: date stamp, 22 August 2010. Blue and black argyle knee socks. Black tights and gray shirt. I'm skating outside at the square, our first practice space. No overhead cover, rough concrete. Our summer home.

Not pictured: the tai chi group who moved in slow unison at one end. The hotel workers who took their dinner breaks on the rock ledges. The small group of women stumbling up and down the square on roller skates.

In the photo I'm skating around an orange cone. Our "track," the orange cones and chalk marks we guessed at every practice. We lined up at one end and skated to the other, hurling ourselves to the ground. Again. Again. Single knee fall. Double knee fall. Plastic knee pad caps scraping concrete. No slide, just clunk.

In the photo my gear is shiny and black. My first pair of wrist guards, long since trash, the yellow helmet strap clean and bright. No stickers. Knee pads duct-tape free, overhead light glinting off plastic. Even my skates look brand new. Bright white laces on my first pair. Fat bell stoppers I couldn't adjust. Couldn't run. No-name black wheels, but they got me around the track.

Behind me there's a skater wearing children's knee pads, black rental skates with tiny wheels and worn-down stoppers. What's her name again? She left without choosing one.

I'm skating around an orange cone in my fresh meat stance. *If you think you're low enough, get lower!* Too tall and too forward.

Socks and nylons date the shot. Knee high stripes and skulls, leopard print tights and polka dots blistered my heels and toes. I switched to athletic pants a few months in, bought packs of men's sports socks. Dry feet and muscle support.

Slideshow. Click. I'm on my ass on the track, near the same cone. My face and chest are shiny with sweat and I'm squinting. Laughing. One leg is bent back, the other forward. Stood up too tall. One foot slip. Fell on my ass. What's new? Tonight, I threw a hit on a jammer. She hit back and I crashed hard on my knees. I practiced hip checks with the fresh meat, clipped wheels and tripped. Last week I took a massive check that knocked me back. I landed bang on one butt-cheek and groaned to my feet.

Falling: nothing new and nothing old. Neither is sweating, indoors or out, we drip all summer long and shiver winters. We skated in that square until mid-November, until snow flurried. Leggings, skirt, t-shirt and hoodie under elbow pads, wrist guards, and gear. Hood up and snot rag around my mouth. Skating laps with ice air cutting into our chests.

But in these photos, it's still hot. Mid-August derby-versary. My start date. Click. My back is facing the photographer in the last shot. Or the first. It's lighter out, early August evening. 12 women in old t-shirts in a line. Bicycle helmets. Skateboard pads. A few are still skating but many have quit. Life got in the way of derby. Derby gets in the way of life. A row of rental skates with duct-taped toes. Shiny new Riedells. A set of rollerblades. We're lined up at the end of the square. *Keep your knees bent, knees bent.* Rules clueless. Bambi on ice. Not letting the wheels slip out from under us.

Another photo. June 3, 2012. Lily and Greta in a wall, pushing me over the inside line, star panty on my head. Still falling. Still clipping skates. Bigger knee pads. Stronger helmets. Uniforms and strategies. But we still fall hard.

the pack

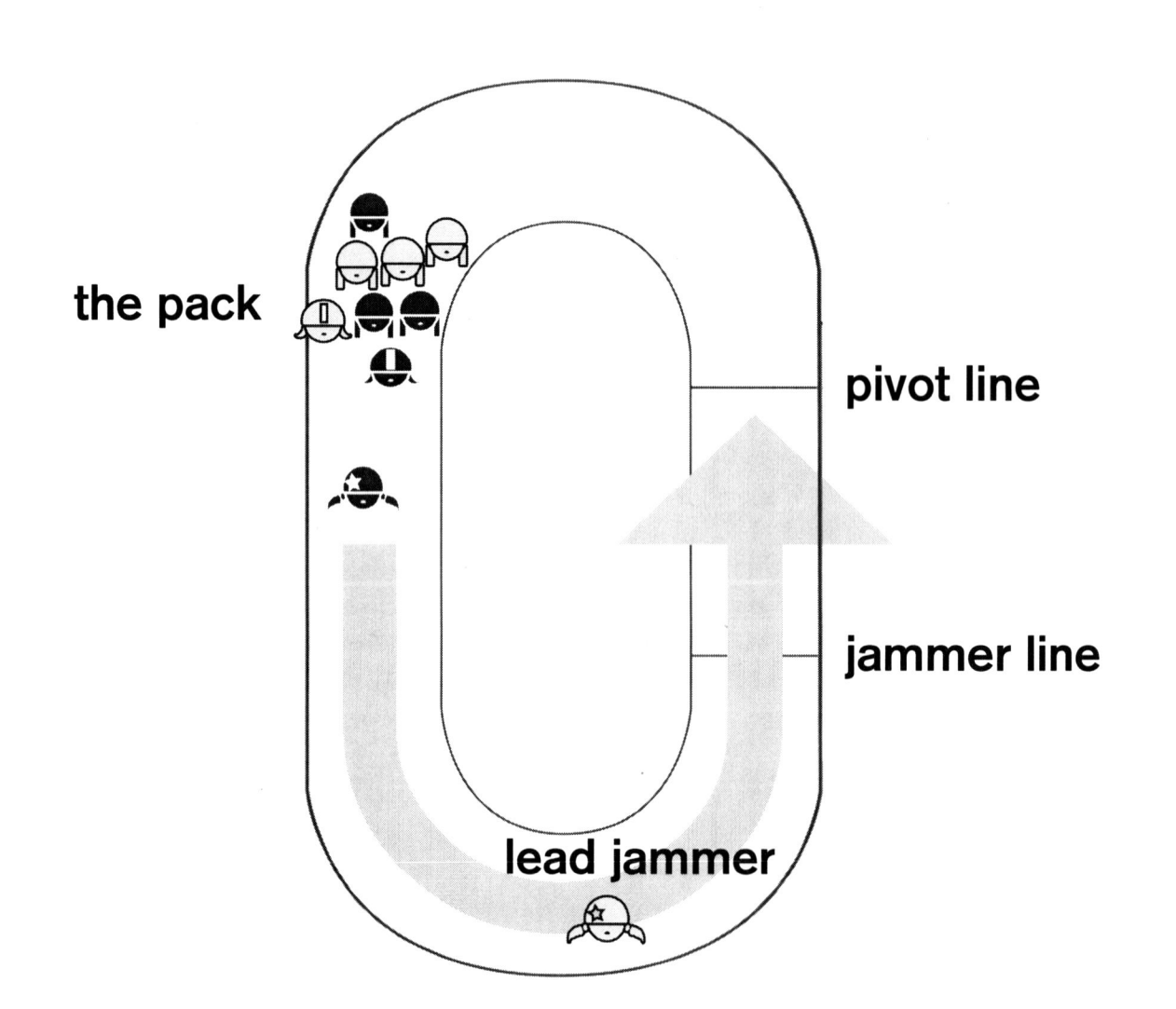

pivot line

jammer line

lead jammer

appendix: roller derby 101

Flat-track roller derby is a complicated sport with a thick rulebook. Bouts are officiated by seven referees, and approximately 14 non-skating officials. With all these people necessary to make sure a bout runs by the book, it's obvious that derby is not the free-for-all many people believe it to be.

The roller derby of today may be based on the derby my parents remember from TV, but game play differs substantially. Today's derby involves mandatory protective equipment and gear checks before each bout, and pays out strict penalties to players who break rules.

Without clotheslining, scripted fights and brawls on the tracks, derby is not any less entertaining. In fact, the real athleticism and skill of its skaters, and the ever-evolving strategies that trickle down from top levels of play, make the sport even more nail-biting for audiences, whether watching from suicide seats next to the track, the stands, or at home live-streaming online.

A roller derby bout consists of two half-hour periods, separated by a half-time break. Each period is broken up into smaller portions called "jams." These jams can last up to a maximum of two-minutes each, but can be substantially shorter. The goal of each team in a jam is to score more points than the opposing team. And how do you do that?

Point scoring works like this:

Each team (barring penalties) fields five skaters per jam, four blockers and a jammer. The jammer is the point-scoring skater on each team, designated by the star helmet panty she wears. Jammers start on the jammer line, thirty feet behind the pivot line. Blockers must start between the jammer and pivot lines. The jam timer blows one whistle and releases the blockers. Once all blockers have crossed the pivot line, two whistle blasts release the jammers (although a new rules revision starting January 2013 releases all blockers and jammers on a single whistle).

The goal of the jammers is to get through the pack (the largest group of blockers from both teams within ten feet of one another) without any penalties as fast as possible. The blockers must help their own jammer while simultaneously stopping the opposing jammer, playing offense and defense at once. Complicated stuff. The first jammer legally out of the pack is called "lead jammer" and can be identified by her jam referee pointing at her as she circles the track. Lead jammer can call off the jam, ending it at any point, by tapping her hands on her hips and will often use this advantage strategically to prevent the other team from scoring points.

The jammers score no points on their first pass through the pack, but begin scoring points for every opposing skater they lap on subsequent passes through the pack. Once the jam is over, the skaters return to their benches, there is a thirty-second break to re-group, and the whole thing starts again. The team with the most points at the end of the bout wins.

While jammers would like to get through the pack by any means possible, and blockers would love to help them do that, there are illegal actions that can send you to the penalty box or even out of the game depending on their severity. Even in this contact sport, contact zones and types of hits are limited. Skaters cannot block to the back of another skater, block above the shoulders or below the knees, or block while stopped or moving clockwise. Other penalties include cutting the track (improving position while skating out of bounds), insubordination, and illegal procedures (starting in the wrong position, false starting, etc.).

Contemporary roller derby only began to gain momentum in the early 2000s, starting in Texas, and spreading across the United States, then into Canada, the United Kingdom, and now around the world. With the sport so new, and leagues springing up at an amazing rate worldwide, strategies and plays are developing quickly, the rules are changing, and the level of play, even in emerging leagues, is always increasing.

This development is part of what makes derby so exciting. It is a new sport. A sport on the move. A sport that only recently hosted its first Roller Derby World Cup, which took place in December 2011 in Toronto, Ontario. Now, potentially vying for a spot in the 2020 Olympic games, roller derby is a sport that can only continue to grow and change with the dedication of its skaters, referees, volunteers and fans.

All that said, I don't pretend to be an expert on roller derby by any means. I'm a relatively new skater who has fallen hard in more ways than one for this sport, and this book is my love letter to roller derby. The vignettes you read here are fictional, but loosely inspired by my experiences as *one* roller derby skater in *one* league in *one* city stumbling my way around the track, through the pack, through the rules, with a smelly gear bag in tow and a group of amazing teammates and crew around me.

glossary

Apex Jump: A move so beautiful when done correctly, that it demands instant replays. When a *jammer* (or a *blocker*, but usually a jammer), leaves both skates to hop the inside line at either apex of the track, shortening her distance and avoiding opposing blockers. When timed wrong, can end in a trip to the *Sin Bin* or the cement.

ASL: American Sign Language.

Blocker: Four out of five skaters on the track (barring penalties) for each team are blockers. Blockers get their *jammers* through the *pack* while simultaneously impeding the other jammer, playing offense and defense at the same time.

Bout: A derby game. Consists of two thirty-minute halves broken into smaller portions called *jams*. Some argue that bouts have a third period: the after-party.

Calling it off: When the *lead jammer* taps her hands on her hips to end the *jam* for strategic reasons. Can be confused by new fans for a rude gesture aimed at the other team.

Cougaring: Also known as poodling, cougaring is "picking up a *minor*" on purpose. In the old rules-set, a skater with three penalties would start a *jam* out of position behind the jam line. Since this skater is not her team's *jammer*, she picks up a fourth penalty, goes to the box and clears her slate.

Crossover: A skating technique that provides maximum speed and involves crossing one leg over the other and pushing with both feet. Initial employment of backwards, clockwise or backwards-clockwise crossovers can result in frequent reliance upon protective gear.

Derby Widow: A skater's real-life romantic partner. So-named because skaters often spend more time with their teammates, on and off the track, than they do with their "real-life" significant other.

Derby Wife: A derby girl's closest derby companion. Skaters tend to see this person more often than any non-derby romantic partner (see *derby widow*).

Fresh Meat (a.k.a. Freshies): Brand new skaters. Sometimes wobbly, often nervous, but always enthusiastic, these skaters are working their way up to passing their minimum skills testing.

Goat: Usually a weaker or slower *blocker* trapped by the opposing team in an effort to slow down the *pack* and allow their *jammer* to rack up more points. Derby girls screaming "get a goat!" at one another are not talking about heading to the local petting zoo after the *bout*.

Grand Slam: When a *jammer* passes all five opposing skaters (including the opposing jammer), picking up five points and a "that's a graaaaaaaaaaaaaaaand slaaaaaaaaam" from the resident announcer.

Jam: Game play is broken up into jams. These last a maximum of two minutes, and can be *called off* before this time by the *lead jammer*.

Jammer: The point-scoring skaters on each team, these ladies wear a target on their heads in the form of the star helmet *panty*. Opposing *blockers* want to hold them back by any legal means possible, while their own jammer tries to run the hell away.

Lead Jammer: The first *jammer* to legally make it out of the pack on the initial pass, earning the advantage of being able to *call off* the jam. The jam ref signals lead jammer by pointing at this skater as she rounds the track. "Not lead jammer" is signaled by a jam ref crossing and un-crossing his/her arms in front of his/her body.

Major: A penalty that results in a trip to the *Sin Bin*.

Minor: Two wrongs don't make a right, and four wrongs (minors) make a *major*. Earned for lesser offenses, minor penalties add up. Pick up four and you're off to the *Sin Bin*. *Jammers* with three minors usually don't jam without *cougaring* to pick up a fourth. New rules introduced in 2013 eliminate minor penalties altogether.

NSO: Those amazing folks who make roller derby *bouts* happen: non-skating officials. They're the people holding up white boards and stopwatches, recording penalties, running the scoreboard, taking stats, and generally making the derby world go round *sans* skates.

Pack: The largest group of *blockers* from both teams within ten feet of one another. It's a *jammer*'s job to get through, and the opposing *blockers*' job to make sure she doesn't. Blockers can only obstruct and assist while within twenty feet of the *pack*.

Panty: Not as sexy as it sounds. A helmet covering made of stretchy fabric. *Jammers* wear a panty with a star on each side. *Pivots* wear a stripe down the centre of their helmet. The source of many bad jokes at practice (who has my panties? I want your panties. Does anyone have the panties? I could go on…)

Pivot: These skaters tend to have big mouths and are great at pushing their teammates around to get them into position. Listen to your pivot, or face the consequences on the bench. These ladies know their shit. Pivots wear a striped helmet *panty*. They can also quickly become *jammers* in the event of a *star pass*.

Power Jam: A *jam* with only one *jammer* on the track. Usually occurs when the other jammer is stuck in the *Sin Bin* and can help the team at advantage rack up lots of points in a short period of time.

Quads (a.k.a. Quad Skates): Skates with four wheels in a square, rather than a straight line like in-line skates. Derby skates operate on the same general principal but are quite different from the high-top quads you rented from the roller rink at your birthday party 20 years ago.

Sin Bin: Slang for the penalty box.

Skate Tool: Lose a *toe stopper*? *Trucks* too tight? Gotta change wheels? You need a skate tool. And if you need a skate tool, chances are you don't have one. Most are X or T shaped with various ends to fit different sized nuts with a wrench for your stoppers.

Star Pass: A somewhat rarely-employed strategy wherein the *jammer* takes off her star helmet *panty* and hands it to the *pivot* in the middle of a *jam*. Once the pivot puts the star panty on her head, she becomes the jammer for her team. Can result in dropped panties, and jammer-less teams.

Suicide Seats: The best seats in the house at a derby *bout*: on the floor, trackside, right behind the ref lane. So-named because only fans 18 years and older are permitted to sit suicide for safety reasons. You may end up with a skater in your lap.

Toe Stopper: A skate part that screws into the front of a *quad skate* between the wheels. Used to stop and start, a toe stopper on the track during a *jam* can cause face plants and assorted mass chaos.

Trucks (a.k.a. Plates): Nylon or metal pieces attached to the bottom of a *quad skate* boot. Trucks consist of axles (to keep the wheels on), bushings (or cushions), and other assorted hardware, and create the side-to-side action of quad skates, allowing skaters to lean and turn. Too tight trucks can have you rolling in straight lines only, whereas too loose trucks feel like skating on squirrels. Adjust carefully.

Twenty Five in Five: 25 standard track laps in five minutes. The roller derby skills test standard for speed and endurance. Want to hear groans at practice? Announce that it's time for 25 in 5.

Whip: An assist from your own player. Can be taken from the hips, the shirt, the shorts, the arm, the leg, a belt, or anything else a skater can grab hold of and pull.

Zebra: Affectionate term for referees due to their fondness for black and white stripes. Zebras tend to come in herds of seven. With so much going on, we need that many refs to keep the skaters in check.

acknowledgements

Earlier versions of stories in *Talking Derby* have appeared in *Lead Jammer*, *Blood & Thunder*, *fiveonfive*, *Derby Life* and *Inside Line*.

*   *   *

It's impossible to play roller derby on your own. You could try, but it would look pretty ridiculous. The sport wouldn't exist without the dozens of players, coaches, and other volunteers, including fans that make up each league. In a way—no matter how cheesy it may sound—the same goes for putting a book together. *Talking Derby* couldn't have happened without the support and assistance of many, many people.

Thank you first to Marty Gervais and Black Moss Press for encouraging me to write this book and for taking a chance on me. Thanks also to my editing and publishing team at the University of Windsor, whose enthusiasm—for a sport most had never heard of prior to meeting me—was always infectious. Jineen Abuzaid, Aanand Arya, Haley Dagley, Ashly Flannery, Luke Frenette, Miriah Grondin, Lyna Hijazi, Danielle Latendresse, Shelby Maia, Sarah Passingham, Jason Rankin, Lauren Sharpe, Lauren Soul, Nicole Turner, and Karly Van Puymbroeck: I am grateful for all your hard work in getting this book ready for publication.

A big thank you also must go out to Josh Kolm, who provided invaluable edits and suggestions, and calmed my nerves as this process went forward, as well as Nicole Markotić for always supporting my writing and for providing input on many aspects of this work. Thanks also to my brother Stephen Hargreaves for lending his graphic design expertise and knowledge to the design process.

Of course, I can't write a book about roller derby without my roller derby league. The Border City Brawlers have become my derby family and I am indebted to them for their love, support, friendship, knowledge and of course, many bruises. I'd also especially like to thank the skater who introduced me to derby and taught me essentially everything I know about skating. Hooli, I owe you way more than a line in a book.

Thank you to my derby idols who not only motivate me to get on the track every practice, but who graciously agreed to read this book in advance and provide feedback: Bonnie D. Stroir, Scald Eagle, Georgia W. Tush, Luludemon, as well as author Rosemary Nixon and author and derby skater Pamela Ribon, your support for this project is appreciated more than you can imagine.

And last but certainly not least, to the people who may not be part of the derby world, but still support (read: put up with) my roller derby life. To my friends, thank you for understanding and not getting too annoyed when I go on and on about jam starts and penalties, have to cancel on movie nights or show up for parties smelling like a gym bag. To my derby widow, who is always there with a back rub for aching muscles, or a sign of support at the bout, and to my parents who watch me play through their fingers, but never ask me to stop. Thank you all.

Derby love.

Kate "Pain Eyre" Hargreaves is a roller derby skater and writer in Windsor, Ontario, where she works in literary publishing. She holds an MA in English and Creative Writing, and her work has appeared in magazines and anthologies across Canada and the United States.